Amelie at the Window

Amelie at the Window

Penny Rogers

Bridge House

British Library Cataloguing in Publication Data
A Record of this Publication is available from the British
Library

ISBN 978-1-914199-92-9

This edition published 2025 by Bridge House Publishing
Manchester, England

Cover illustrations © Roger Dale

Story illustrations © Roger Dale, Katharine Dew

Amelie at the Window

Penny Rogers

Bridge House

British Library Cataloguing in Publication Data
A Record of this Publication is available from the British
Library

ISBN 978-1-914199-92-9

This edition published 2025 by Bridge House Publishing
Manchester, England

Cover illustrations © Roger Dale

Story illustrations © Roger Dale, Katharine Dew

To my grandson James Dew.
Perhaps one day he'll make the film.

Contents

Foreword

Amelie at the Window began as a short story written in 2014. The response from readers was positive and unanimous; they wanted to read more about Amelie and her world. Slowly the stories about her life, her hopes and dreams, emerged. At the same time the other characters developed, some in ways that were almost predestined but some able to take advantage of the changes in society brought about by World War 1. This was especially true for the women, their aspirations beginning to be realised as they gradually widened their roles in society.

So, *Amelie at the Window* is essentially a collection of short stories about the people who lived in a fictional small town, somewhere in France, in 1914 and again in 1924. Each story takes the reader deeper into the lives of the town's inhabitants, and the reader will find the same event described and recalled in several ways by different people. This is why the voices in the stories are not consistent through the book. In some stories there is a clear narrative from an individual, giving their perspectives and recollections of events. In others, readers will find more than one view of the same event and in one instance the story is told in the first person. Why this voice has been chosen for this character could perhaps be a question for a reading group discussion.

PART 1

1914

Amelie at the Window

Christophe Pichon was still there. The blurry glow emanating from the gas lights in the dairy across La Place de la République made him look so handsome. Amelie sighed. She was in love. The October afternoon had turned into a chilly evening; it was 6.30 and almost dark. By the dim light of the dairy she watched the young man shuffle from foot to foot. The story of how his left foot had been broken when he was a lad, riding the greengrocer's horse as a dare, was still a source of amusement in the town. '*Pauvre Christophe,*' she said softly, 'you need boots that fit properly and don't hurt your feet. And when we're married they won't dare laugh at you.'

She knew that Christophe had been outside the dairy for almost an hour. She wondered who, or what, he was waiting for. At least she could see him and dream about standing next to him. She wriggled in her chair, willing her wasted legs to move. Soon Odille would come to put her to bed. Oh the indignities of it all! She closed her eyes and imagined Christophe carrying her downstairs and out into the world. He would take her to Lourdes, she just knew he would. When she was cured and able to walk he would marry her as soon as possible. They would always be happy together and never ignore each other as her parents did.

A shout from the other side of the square caught Amelie's attention. M and Mme Fischer were arguing. They usually had a row after the second or third absinthe, but today they had at least four before the tension began to build. She knew that Raymond Fischer had come to the town as a young man, running away from something, or someone, in his native Alsace. His curious accent amused Amelie; she knew that behind his back the locals called him *choucroute*. She also knew they never dared call him that to his face, he had a bad temper and a short fuse, although the years and alcohol had slowed him down.

In the room above the milliner's shop, Amelie picked up her sewing. Needlework was her escape, her link to the world beyond her window. She embroidered appliqués for the hats her parents sold and did a little work on commission. At the moment she was embroidering a velvet cape. It was difficult to hold the slippery material secure in the hoop without damaging the fabric. Slowly a profusion of exotic birds was transforming the edge of the cape. She picked up her work, but it was too dark to see properly. The parrot's wing would have to wait until the morning.

Amelie could hear voices coming from the shop below. The words were muffled and indistinct but she gathered that Mme Gaudin was undecided about the inclusion of an ostrich feather in her new hat. Amelie strained her ears to catch more of the conversation. Mme Gaudin had seen in an illustrated paper, that peacock feathers were in vogue this year and she wanted to be up to date with the fashion. On the other hand she did not want to appear ostentatious in the *endroit reculé* of Forentan. Amelie was horrified to hear her home town referred to as a backwater, and she guessed her parents would be as well. But Mme Gaudin was a good customer, so there was nothing they could do except agree, suggest, agree and suggest.

Another shout from across the street caused Amelie to re-focus on the deteriorating situation outside the *tabac*. After several drinks they started arguing, inevitably about Clovis. Amelie vaguely recalled the red-haired infant son of Marie-Pierre Fischer. He had died of polio during the same outbreak that had killed many children and left her with legs that didn't work. According to Odille, a young woman employed by her mother as a part-time nurse and carer, Clovis was born just two months after the Fischers' wedding. Odille had said that although the child wasn't his, Raymond Fischer had treated him as his own, doted on him and was heartbroken when he died. Odille reckoned that Marie-Pierre's heart had broken as well, and that they both drank so much to hide their pain.

Most evenings Amelie watched the altercations between the Fischers with a combination of horror and amusement, but tonight her attention was divided between the *tabac* and the dairy. Her eyes were fixed on the latter until it was too dark for her to see the angelic profile of her beloved. She vaguely wondered where Odille had got to; she wasn't usually late. Below she heard her mother saying *'Au revoir'* and *'Merci beaucoup'* to Mme Gaudin. Then the sound of Maman trudging up the stairs. She saw Papa cross the street and hurry to the dairy. To her amazement he was soon in conversation with the adored Christophe.

Her concentration on the unusual sight of her father talking to the man she intended to marry was broken by shouting from the *tabac*. She saw Marie-Pierre pick up a chair and smack it across the head of the inebriated Raymond. Blood and invectives flowed across the square. Amelie did not know whether to watch the drama with the Fischers unfold or keep her eyes on Christophe and her father.

Her dilemma was solved when Maman came into her room. 'Odille won't be coming any more. I'll have to care for you myself until we can find someone else.' Amelie's heart sank. Her mother was never gentle. More importantly, Odille was her source of information, a bridge to the world beyond her bedroom: news of events, gossip, even salacious titbits that had to be whispered when Maman was not around.

'What's the matter with Odille?' she ventured.

Maman sniffed. 'No better than she ought to be.' Amelie watched as her mother busied with preparations for bed. She could hear Maman muttering *'catin'* and *'prostituée'*.

Amelie was none the wiser but didn't want to upset her mother even more by asking questions.

As the autumn dusk turned rapidly to dark, a few more gas lights were lit. Amelie stayed glued to the window until the last possible moment. She wished with all her heart that she knew what Christophe and her father were talking about.

Her concentration on the two men was distracted by the sight of a horse and cart trundling around the square. From her vantage point Amelie could recognise all the locals and their horses, carts, bicycles, even the occasional automobile. But she'd never seen this before. She felt very sorry for the horse, it looked worn-out and dejected. Then she noticed what it was pulling, a sort of trailer with what looked like a wooden shed crazily fixed to the flat bed. Her first thought was that it must be a circus! How exciting, perhaps she could go to that and see the wild animals. Then she made out the faded words on the side of the cart. It was a travelling photographer. *Quelle déception.*

She turned her attention back to the scene outside the dairy. Christophe was hopping from one foot to the other; her father was punching his fist into the palm of his other hand. He always did this when he was arguing. Amelie considered that this did not bode well for Christophe; her father frequently argued and never conceded anything.

Meanwhile outside the *tabac*, the nightly charade of the Fischers had ended. Amelie watched the husband and wife making their way home with considerable difficulty. Raymond could hardly walk; the arms of his wife, strengthened by a lifetime of hard work, held him just about upright. She guessed, correctly, that the proprietor Bernard Lavoisier was telling them, as he told them almost every day, that they weren't to come back, that their custom was not worth the fuss and that they would have to pay for the chair. In truth the chair was fine. Raymond's head less so.

15

Amelie looked back towards the dairy just in time to see Christophe step back from her father and shake his head. Then he seemed to hesitate, turn and move towards the older man before reluctantly holding out his hand. The two men shook hands then turned away from each other. How she wished that she could have heard what they had been talking about.

At 7.25 Amelie was in bed with a bowl of hot chocolate placed carefully on the table beside her. Her mother had clearly resented the wiping, the washing, the holding, the lifting and the dressing. But Amelie closed her eyes and dreamed of the future, WALKING down the aisle with the man of her dreams.

In her room above her parents' shop, Amelie drifted off to sleep. She wondered why her evening chocolate always tasted so much better than the insipid drink she had in the morning; one day she'd pluck up the courage to ask her mother. But for now she slept, dreaming of the day she would become Madame Pichon.

Outside the *Tabac*

More and more alcohol was needed to help the Fischers cope with their loss. Bernard knew Marie-Pierre was drinking too much, but what could he do? He owed her a lot, and although he had never admitted it, he loved her. He picked up an old copy of *Le Figaro*. Every page had something about the war with Germany. He was forty-four, just young enough to enlist. He pondered once more the prospect of joining the army, reasoning he had nothing to lose and it would give him a way out of Forentan. There was nothing to keep him in the town: no wife, no family, just a run-down café that just about made ends meet.

The clock above the untidy counter told him it was just after 7.00. That snooty Mme Gaudin from the Manoir was leaving the hat shop at long last. He guessed that Lemonnier would soon be over for his package. He must have seen the carrier's cart arrive early that morning. Now Bernard knew why every few months the package arrived for the milliner. He really wished he didn't.

Mme Gaudin was taking her time, and the Lemonniers were probably trying to get rid of her. Serve them all right, thought Bernard. He had no time for any of them. Then he thought about Amelie. She would be sitting all alone in that dark room above the shop. Poor kid. He sometimes saw her in the summer when she was carried downstairs and pushed round the town in an invalid chair. This happened more when she was smaller, but less so now she was fifteen and a grown woman. He could see it must be difficult to get her up and down the steep stairs between the shop and the upstairs apartment. When the girl had finally been manhandled into the invalid chair the narrow, cobbled streets of the town made it impossible to take her far. He could see that Amelie found the experience undignified and desperately uncomfortable. He remembered her as a pretty little thing, dancing in the sunshine. He used to think that his Rosalie would have looked like that had she lived. Then in the summer of 1908 when she was nine, Amelie contracted polio as well. Bernard wondered if she'd have been better off not recovering, only to spend the rest of her life as a prisoner in that room over the shop. The thought of those parcels for her father made Bernard shudder.

The fourth absinthe had been too much for the Fischers.

'For the last time, stop swearing.' Bernard knew his pleas would make no difference, and yet again he vowed to never serve them again.

'Whore!' yelled Raymond.

'Don't call me that, you lazy good-for-nothing-German.' Marie-Pierre sneered at him; she knew full well that he was French.

'It's your fault Clovis died,' retorted Raymond. 'Paying more attention to your fancy man and his kids than you did to your own son.'

Before Bernard could do anything to stop her, Marie-Pierre had picked up an iron chair, lifted it high above her head and smacked it down on her husband's skull. Raymond crumpled. '*Mon Dieu,* you've killed him!' shouted Bernard.

Marie-Pierre scooped up her husband. 'He'll be alright. Take more than a knock to kill the old goat.' And with that she half carried and half dragged him across the square towards their squalid basement room.

Bernard got a cloth to clear up the mess outside his *tabac*. In the gloom he saw Lemonnier making his way towards the dairy. To no one in particular he said, 'Why is he going there and not coming here for his parcel?' He turned round to get a better view and saw the milliner deep in conversation with Christophe Pichon. They were too far away for him to hear what was being said, so he busied himself with clearing up after the Fischers.

About twenty minutes later Lemonnier left Pichon and walked purposefully towards the café. Bernard resigned himself to the fact that he wouldn't say anything about the pornography he had seen in the damaged package. He could not afford to lose any custom, and though the milliner wasn't a big spender he had influence in the town. Times were hard, so when the torn package had arrived that morning he'd toyed with the idea of confronting Lemonnier with the contents but came to think the better of it. The package had been wrapped in an old feed sack and vermin must have chewed through the damaged hessian to get at some residual grain inside it. So Bernard had re-tied the package and stuck some sealing wax roughly over the worst tear in the covering. It looked odd, but it was the best he could do.

Lemonnier inspected the result. He leered towards Bernard. 'If you want to see them, just ask. I've got plenty more in my office.'

The Way Out

Marcel had gone with his mother to help her with the errands. He hoped that his father wouldn't come home early from work and find out that he was helping her. She was very tired and very pregnant, and all he did for her was carry heavy things, open doors and make sure that the little ones who came with them didn't stray too far or get into mischief. The trouble was that François Durand did not approve of men doing what he considered women's work. 'That's your mother's job,' he'd growl whenever Marcel tried to help her. The fact that she was about to bring yet another baby into the world made no difference. He often wondered how his mother would manage when he had left. He supposed that his sister Monique would do more, but she had enough to do looking after the animals and cultivating the garden. His next sister, Joséphine, was simple. She tried to help but was clumsy, forgot what she was doing and it took so long to put things right after she'd helped that generally it was better to keep her out of the way. The younger girls did their bit, but none of them would be much use to their mother when the next baby arrived.

Marcel had always assumed that he'd follow his father into a job with horses at the Manoir where François had looked after the horses since he was a boy. He knew everything about them, giving both the thoroughbreds and the draught horses the same skilled care. But the horses were gone, sent off to the front. Even old Dolores who had taught all the children to ride had been herded onto a train with dozens of others. Marcel knew now that he would never follow his father into a job, he also understood that Papa might not have a job for much longer now that there were no horses to care for.

This uncertainty made Marcel determined to enlist when the recruiting officer came to Forentan. He would be able to send money to his mother; perhaps she would then be able to afford to pay someone to help her. He would no longer be a strain on the limited family income. He'd have a free uniform, free boots, free board and lodgings. According to a man that his friend Christophe had met when he went to Le Cellet to collect a parcel for the milliner Lemonnier, the army have doctors and dentists who sort out all your illnesses for nothing. *Tout gratuit*. Marvellous.

Marcel and his mother shepherded the little ones into the bakery.

'*Bonsoir*, Monsieur Joubert. Two loaves please. I don't mind if they were from this morning's batch.'

Marcel knew exactly what was meant by this. He knew that the baker always made sure he had some 'stale' bread for the Durands. When Mme Joubert had been very ill his mother had nursed her, and it was widely accepted that she had saved her life. Marcel had long been aware that his mother always reciprocated the baker's generosity with a plump rabbit at Easter, and eggs when the hens were laying well.

'Would any child in my shop like a madeleine?' The little Durands crowded around the baker as he dramatically produced small treats from a bag on the table in front of him.

'Say thank you,' instructed their mother.

'*Merci, Monsieur*.' The voices were more or less in unison. 'Can we take one for Joséphine?' asked a small boy.

'Of course, but don't eat it yourself on the way home.'

It was many years since Marcel had enjoyed a treat from the baker. His idea of a treat now was to see the world, to go beyond the confines of a run-down town and experience new things. Even meet some girls.

As they trooped out of the bakery an old cart trundled past them. In spite of the fading light, it was clear that both the horse and the once-elaborate trailer that it pulled were on their last legs. From the faded writing on the side nearest to him, Marcel could see that it was a travelling photographer. Not a good business to be in. Some people had their own Kodak Brownie these days, even in Forentan, and if they wanted a portrait done to celebrate a wedding or anniversary then there was a studio in Le Cellet. Marcel looked with sadness at the dejected scene. It summed up exactly what was wrong with his life. He needed to move on, not become stuck in a rut and unable to do anything different. In the few minutes it took for the photographer's cart to rumble up the street Marcel made his firm decision. Tomorrow he'd tell his mother that he was going to join the army.

On the other side of La Place de la République a racket caught everyone's attention. It was the worryingly predictable outbreak of hostilities between Marie-Pierre and Raymond Fischer. Bernard, the owner of the small *tabac*, was trying to silence the warring couple. 'He shouldn't serve them so many absinthes,' opined Mme Durand. Marcel was trying to stop his little siblings from hearing the foul language and insults that were being traded by the Fischers when a mighty crack ended all the shouting. Marie-Pierre had whacked her husband over the head with an iron chair, felling him like a tree onto the cobbles outside the *tabac*.

'*Retournons-nous*; we need to go home.' Marcel's mother attempted to marshal her flock back up the street. But this entertainment was too good to miss. All eyes were glued to the prostrate form of Raymond and the sight of his wife still holding the heavy chair above her head.

'You've killed him.' Bernard's shout broke the silence that had initially followed the shouting and sound of chair on bone. Marie-Pierre put the chair down, said something to Bernard then picked up her husband and staggered off towards their basement rooms with Raymond bleeding profusely, leaving a trail of blood across the square.

On the other side of the square Marcel spotted his friend Christophe, evidently waiting for someone outside the dairy. Christophe wanted to enlist as well; the two had planned this for some time. Now Christophe's girl had told him they had to get married, there was a baby on the way. Marcel knew that his friend was being conned: kissing did not make a girl pregnant. But Christophe was gullible and wanted to do the honourable thing. Marcel thought he'd have another attempt to make his friend see sense.

'*Maman*, can you manage to get home OK? Is there too much to carry? I'd like to stay and have a word with Christophe.'

'*Merci mon cher*, I can manage.'

'Don't be late!' she called as she plodded off with her shopping and assorted children.

Marcel walked towards the pool of light outside the dairy. Christophe had been standing there for some time and was clearly uncomfortable, shifting from foot to foot and looking intently towards the hat shop opposite him.

'How are you doing?' Marcel called out to his friend. Christophe ignored him. Marcel saw why as he spotted Gaston Lemonnier leaving his millinery shop and walking purposefully towards the dairy. He knew that Christophe did odd jobs for Lemonnier; perhaps he had some work that he wanted doing. The creepy old milliner was another reason why Marcel wanted to leave Forentan. Everyone, including his mother, held Lemonnier in high esteem, said he was 'respectable'. But Marcel knew different. He never said anything to anyone, but one day he'd been scrambling along the roof at the back of the hat shop looking for a pigeon that he'd shot with a catapult, and he'd seen what the milliner did in his office.

So Marcel hung back, keeping in the shadows and listening to the conversation. He was amazed by the gullibility of his friend. Odille was not pregnant; she couldn't be. Marcel could not understand why she would make up this story, but he did know his friend was being duped. So Marcel made another decision. With or without Christophe he would enlist. The army was the only way out.

Getting Ready for Bed

'*Merci beaucoup Madame Gaudin, au revoir, Madame.*'
As the last customer left the milliner's shop, M Gaston
Lemonnier walked out of the rear door without so much as
a word or acknowledgement to his wife. She slowly closed
the shutters and locked up the shop.

Mme Christine Lemonnier looked in the mirror. She
fought back the tears; she had no time for self-pity. The face
that stared back looked considerably older than her thirty-five
years. The illness was now visibly taking its toll. She
considered, not for the first time, that if Gaston was any sort
of real husband he would have noticed long ago. With no one
to confide in she was going to have to deal with this on her
own. The war with Germany was already making every aspect
of life more difficult; she dreaded what 1915 would bring.

She began the slow and painful climb up the stairs. Poor
little Amelie – there was only one thing she could do for
her crippled daughter. She knew she'd have to act soon, the
cancer was spreading and she couldn't leave her daughter
in the care of Gaston. The announcement earlier today from
Odille that she was going to have a child had been a
complete surprise. Privately Christine did not believe the
girl, but she couldn't imagine why she should make up such
a story. Her reputation was now in shreds, what was the
point of deliberately doing that?

Meanwhile she was going to have to care for Amelie, and
she barely had the strength to care for herself and finish hats
for the few customers that still came into the shop. Business
was slow, and she could see no prospect of it picking up.

In Amelie's room she watched her daughter for a few
seconds. She was peering out of the window, watching that
Christophe Pichon. Silly girl. Fleetingly she remembered
how it felt to be fifteen years old, with so much to look
forward to. For Christine the future had been a loveless

marriage, hard work and a sick daughter. She knew that for Amelie the future would be very different.

In the fading light Christine's eye was caught by a movement on the other side of the square. An old horse pulling a shabby cart trundled up the road and past the church. What did it remind her of? Her mind went back to a warm, spring evening eight or nine years previously when a travelling photographer had set up in the square. She had had several portraits done of Amelie. The little girl had found it difficult to keep still; all she wanted to do was skip. The pictures were kept out of sight these days, a sad reminder of a girl who once danced and now could not even walk.

Amelie was still fixated on the view from her window. Christine started to collect up the clothes and cloths she would need for the task that lay ahead. She really ought to bring some hot water up the stairs, but the prospect of going back downstairs, heating the water and then carrying it up to wash her daughter was more than she could manage. The desperation of her situation hit her as never before.

Christine had already spoken to the Mother Superior. Tomorrow she would have to go and see Père Dujardin. That would mean telling him about her illness, but it would have to be done. He would ask her about Gaston; that was the difficult bit. How could she explain why she could not leave a daughter with her own father? Christine knew that she ought to involve Gaston. Tell him about her illness and discuss with him the best course of action for their only child. But she couldn't bring herself to even talk to him; the gulf between them was unbridgeable. Her husband was sullen and unpredictable, and she shuddered as she thought of the pictures she had found while cleaning his office.

'*Maman*, what's the matter with Odille?'

Christine replied to the girl in as few words as possible. Long practice of being terse and uncommunicative had cut down the possibility of having to answer unwanted questions.

'No better than she ought to be. It's cold water tonight; there wasn't time to heat any.'

Amelie shrugged, as if resigned to the prospect of a cold wash.

The next few days would be very difficult. If Gaston had any idea of her plans she was sure he would thwart them. No, Amelie had to be safely out of the way before she told her husband. What he would do then she had no idea, but at least the child would be spared his anger and violence. She doubted that he would try to bring his daughter home, but she could not be certain. Mère Agnès had suggested that it might be better if the invalid novice went to Louche-la-Mustique, some way away. The convent there was on one level, making it more suitable for an invalid chair to be pushed around. Neither woman mentioned the advantage of having some distance between Amelie and her father, or indeed her dying mother. This unspoken understanding between them was the only support that Christine received during the whole painful process.

Shouting from the other side of the square sent Christine hurrying to the window. By the dim light of the gas lamp outside the *tabac* she could see Raymond Fischer lying on the ground and Marie-Pierre waving her arms about over him. She turned away, shocked to see what had become of her old friend.

She considered Marie-Pierre; they had attended the convent school together and had been friends. Then the silly girl had ruined her life when she fell for the Irish mercenary who'd appeared in the town. She had never seen anyone with red hair before, and before long the town was buzzing with news of her pregnancy. The soldier disappeared as quickly as he had arrived, leaving Marie-Pierre to make what she could of the situation. It seemed that Raymond Fischer was the best she could do. He wanted to make a permanent home for himself in Forentan and she needed some semblance of respectability.

'What would you think if I asked Mme Fischer to help

27

me look after you?' The question was out of Christine's mouth before she realised it.

'But, *Maman*, she is always drunk. I've just seen her hit her husband with a chair. I think she might have killed him!' Amelie turned round in her chair to look at her mother. Being asked her opinion was most unusual, and Mme Fischer seemed an unlikely candidate to care for her.

'I would ensure that this did not happen. *Ma cherie*, Mme Fischer is very strong and she is also very kind. I have known her for many years. She will not drink when she is helping us.' Her use of 'us' seemed to startle Amelie, as if she didn't believe her mother needed help.

'As you wish, *Maman*.' Maybe it was too much for her daughter to take in: asking what she thought, intimating that she needed help, calling her '*Ma cherie*', all on top of her father talking to Christophe. Did Amelie sense that change was in the air?

Christine was beginning to see a way out of her predicament. She allowed herself a small, secret smile. Following her daughter's unrelenting gaze across the square, she was surprised to see young Pichon in deep conversation with Gaston outside of the dairy. What is going on? she mused. What are they talking about? It occurred to Christine that if her husband was up to something it might make her task of spiriting their daughter out of town a little bit easier. She drew the curtains, wondering if Marie-Pierre could help her do what she had to without Gaston knowing, and turned the oil lamp down to its lowest setting.

Christine painfully descended the stairs to make Amelie her evening bowl of hot chocolate. She watched the hard black chocolate melt, slowly at first then faster as the heat increased. Carefully she stirred in the sugar and the milk; she added a generous measure of brandy. By the time she had finished the task her mind was made up. Tomorrow she would talk to Marie-Pierre, and then she would go to see Père Dujardin.

The brandy would ensure her daughter got a good night's sleep. Tomorrow she would have to tell Amelie about Odille and her inevitable marriage to Christophe. Back in the gloomy bedroom she put the bowl of chocolate where her daughter could reach it. 'Drink up and sleep well.' Christine saw Amelie's smile and wished for the briefest of moments that they had had a closer, more demonstrative, relationship. But it was foolish to think like this. She allowed herself to hold her daughter's hand.

'*Bonne nuit, Maman.*'

With sadness and resignation she looked at her daughter in bed, her beautiful dark brown hair, her sweet face, and her delicate hands peeping out over the coverlet. Christine Lemonnier had to leave the room very quickly; it was almost too much to bear.

Evening Penance

Père Michel Dujardin opened the door of the presbytery. It was 6.30, time for his evening penance. He was dreading having to kneel on the hard, cold floor but what could he do? He had vowed to do this and he was not a man to break his word, especially a promise made to the Heavenly Father. Twenty years ago it had seemed a reasonable response to a minor transgression; the priest had long since forgotten what he had done, or more likely not done, but at 6.30 every evening he prayed to atone for a long-forgotten sin in the sanctuary of his dilapidated church.

It was only October, but the autumn storms had made the roof leak even more and Père Dujardin wondered what would happen when the weight of snow settled on it. He had asked the bishop many times for help with the repair of the church, but the bishop in his wisdom kept well away from the affairs of Forentan. It was common knowledge among the clergy in the area that the bishop now had a motor car, a De Dion Bouton apparently, painted in maroon with black leather seats. No one outside the city had seen this marvel, but it was understood by everyone that it was essential for the bishop to keep in touch with ecclesiastical business.

Arthritic knees on cold church floors are a painful combination, and the priest wondered if the Lord Almighty would object to the insertion of a hassock between his limbs and the relentless chill of the tiles. Perhaps if he could remember what he'd done wrong he could end this daily penance.

So he prayed, trying to forget the pain in his knees by imagining the torture of the Saviour on the cross of Calvary. 'Lord, please give me guidance. Next week I am to marry a young couple. My housekeeper tells me that the girl is with child, but my instinct questions this. Heavenly father, I am not a man of the venal world, how can I know the truth? Am I being deceived? Please show me how to deal with this dilemma.'

As the evening darkened outside Père Dujardin carried on with his devotions, his knees now numb with the cold. 'I pray for peace. This war with Germany is gathering momentum and I cannot think how it will end. The news from the eastern front is not good; many men are lost every day. There will be recruitment here in a fortnight and I fear all our young men will go. Then who will work the fields?' As he contemplated the effects of the war, he thought of Raymond Fischer. He felt sorry for the man; no one liked him and now he was becoming the brunt of anti-German sentiments in the town. Père Michel had pointed out to more than one of his parishioners that M Fischer was French, he had grown up speaking Alsatian but he was not German. Silently the priest considered the narrow line between patriotism and nationalism and wondered if he could incorporate something about it into a sermon. He quickly decided against it; after all, he needed money to repair the church.

The priest wondered how to raise the subject of the roof. Clearly the Almighty could not be expected to sort out such mundane problems, but Dujardin reassured himself that as God was omnipotent then it was not unreasonable to include this vital request that was so important to his servant in Forentan. 'There is little money in the town, no rich benefactor I can turn to. Your house is in need of repair. With your guidance I can attempt to satisfy the spiritual needs of your flock, but without money I cannot maintain the building.' Père Dujardin thought that anything further on this matter would be presumptuous, so he turned to something rather different.

The problem of the long-forgotten sin came into his mind. He reasoned that if he could recall this old misdemeanour he could fully atone for it and cease this nightly ritual that was causing him so much pain. His mind wandered back to his days in the seminary when he was a young man, passionate about his calling to serve God. What had happened so long ago to make him do this?

He shifted on the cold floor, trying to ease the pain in his knees. 'Any day now the milliner will be coming to make his confession. I have told him to cease his practice of looking at images that he would not wish his priest to see. At every confession he tells me that he will stop, that he will burn all that he has and not acquire any new ones, yet every eight weeks or so he is back, with yet more salacious thoughts to confess. I wonder if these confessions are part of his pleasure. He says the Hail Marys as I instruct him and he assures me that he reads the psalms as a distraction from the enticements of the devil, but it seems to no avail. Please guide him to the path of virtue, and help me to listen to his predilections and not be corrupted by them.'

The priest turned his thoughts to the milliner's crippled daughter. Amelie seldom came to church these days. He had asked her mother why she came so rarely. Mme Lemonnier's reply was guarded. She said that the girl was getting too big to carry down the stairs from the apartment above the shop. Dujardin looked at the woman, noticing how thin she was, nothing but skin and bone. 'So she is there all the time?'

'And what else am I supposed to do?' was the frosty reply. 'It is no longer possible for me to carry her down the stairs.'

He wondered whether to suggest that M Lemonnier might be able to help, but thought the better of it. Poor Amelie, mused the priest, but at least she was warm and well-fed, not like the scabby urchins who roamed around the town begging and stealing to survive. His kindly nature made Dujardin want to help these *gamins*, but common sense in the form of his housekeeper told him that to feed and clothe these wretched children would only encourage indolence and make the problem worse.

There were many large families in his parish and the bounty of God to bestow such fecundity was a source of unresolved conflict in the priest's mind. On the one hand he firmly believed the words he uttered many times every day, 'Thy will be done', but he also saw the misery caused by too many children with not enough food to eat. He also saw the dangers of childbirth; he had buried many women and even more babies who had not survived. He thought of Mme Durand. She must be near her time. He prayed for the safe delivery of her child and he prayed for the souls of the twins she had borne a few years ago; both little girls had died before they could be baptised. The local *sage-femme*, the redoubtable Mme Fachon, who was booked to attend Mme Durand, had assured him that should the baby be sickly she would send for him immediately. Père Dujardin resolved to sleep with his clothes on and everything he needed by the side of his bed, just in case he was called. He prayed that his preparations would not be needed.

Afterwards he considered that a miracle happened that evening. Alone in the damp cold of his beloved but decrepit church he knelt on his worn-out knees. Through the silence he heard a voice that he recognised immediately as belonging to Père Julien, the long deceased head of the seminary.

'*Frère Michel*, time to stop this you know. You were always late for vespers; I recall that you were so engrossed in your books that you forgot the time and didn't hear the bell. I think that by now you have learnt that God is more important than your studies. You must move on.'

Of course, that was it! The relieved priest prayed for his departed mentor in the realisation that this was the last time he would endure the torture of the unforgiving floor. He allowed his mind to wander away from the damp church and

33

into the warmth of his study. The fire would be lit by now, crackling in the hearth and illuminating his shabby room with its flickering light. Tonight he would treat himself to a cognac; the Lord had answered one of his questions.

His final hour of penance was coming to a close. Through the windows he could see only blackness. A solitary candle burned beside him, and by its faltering light he took out his pocket watch. The hands pointed to 7.28. With considerable relief and with great fervour he prayed out loud. 'Hail Mary, full of grace, the Lord is with thee; blessed art thou amongst women, and blessed is the fruit of thy womb, Jesus.'

The priest gritted his teeth and for the last time began the slow and agonising process of rising from the floor.

The Power of Prayer

Mme Hortense Durand shifted uneasily. Her back hurt, she needed to get home. After twelve confinements she knew the signs. She watched her little ones enjoy their treats from the baker. He was a good man. Over the years she'd helped him, nursed his wife when she almost died from influenza in 1910 and looked after his children while she recovered. And these days he helped her, selling bread to her at a knock-down price and giving *les gamins* biscuits and cakes when they visited the shop.

As the children enjoyed their treats Hortense prayed silently to Mary the Mother of God. 'Holy Mother please guard me through the perils of what is to come. Keep me safe so that I might see my children grow.'

'Come on, everybody, we need to go home.' She kept her voice playful, but she didn't want to waste any time. As they left the shop a dreadful shout erupted from across the square. There was a fight outside Bernard's *tabac*, it had to be the Fischers. All the children gazed in astonishment at the spectacle of Marie-Pierre Fischer standing over the recumbent body of her husband Raymond, an iron chair still held above her head. Her language was blasphemous; Bernard was trying to quieten her but to no avail. Marcel rounded up his brothers and sisters. 'Come on, you lot, let's go home. I expect Papa's back from work by now.' But they ignored their big brother; he didn't have the same clout with them that their mother did.

'Home!' commanded Hortense. 'Do as Marcel tells you.' She looked with affection at the boy. She knew he wanted to enlist; there was no work and no future in Forentan. The army seemed the only way out, but she did not want him to go. He hadn't said anything to her, but she sensed that it was only a matter of time.

Meanwhile she had other things to worry about. Apart

from the baby that was about to be born, François had told her that his job was certain to disappear. The horses at Le Manoir had all been sent to the front – all except one they were keeping to pull the only carriage they had left. Her husband had looked after M Gaudin's horses for most of his life. He had been groom, stud man, vet, driver, breaker, and riding teacher to the Gaudin boys. Now his beloved charges had gone. They both knew they would not return.

But her main concern now was the birth of her baby. Twelve times she had survived childbirth. Not all the babies had. She recalled the freezing February night six years ago when she delivered twins. In spite of the best efforts of the *sage-femme* both the little girls had died before they could be baptised. Hortense prayed for their souls every day. She trusted Mary the blessed Mother of God to help her; her deep religious conviction was a source of strength in everything she did.

'*Maman*, is it OK if I go and have a word with Christophe? Can you manage?' Marcel had seen his pal outside the dairy. Hortense guessed that the two of them were planning to join up together. She'd heard that Christophe's girl was expecting and she wondered if that would make a difference. But she couldn't worry about that now; she had her own confinement to worry about.

'Of course. I'm fine. The kids can carry the bread. Don't be late!' In truth she was relieved that Marcel wasn't going to walk home with her. François had very strong ideas about men doing women's work. He would think it demeaning if he saw his son, his eldest son, walking with his mother carrying the shopping and minding the wayward rabble of excited small children. With everything else she was dealing with, Hortense did not want to have to apologise to her husband.

'Be good for *Maman*,' Marcel exhorted, and made his way across the square.

It wasn't far to the Durands' smallholding on the outskirts of Forentan, but to Hortense on that autumn evening it seemed a long way. The stray pains she'd been experiencing all evening were starting to be more organised, more regular.

She was glad she'd taken a raspberry leaf tisane before she left the house to do the errands. Her store cupboard was well stocked with dried herbs, flowers and roots; there were tisanes, infusions and elixirs for all eventualities and ailments. Perhaps the smoke from burning raspberry leaves would help her through the night? It was worth a try.

'Where's my supper?' François was home, and clearly upset.

'Not long, there's soup on the fire and I've got some bread.'

'No work tomorrow. No work ever for Gaudin. It's over.'

Without a word Hortense brought soup and bread to her husband. She put her hand on his back. 'We'll manage.'

'Don't know how. Where's Marcel?'

'He'll be back soon. Talking to Pichon.'

'No work for him at Le Manoir. Ever.' François put his head in his hands. He looked up at Hortense. He said nothing.

'My time has come.' She took his hand. 'I'll call Monique, ask her to get Mme Fachon.'

'Have you got money for her?' The implications of calling a midwife to assist with a birth she knew had never occurred to François. That was women's business; it had taken seventeen years of marriage, ten surviving children and the imminent thirteenth confinement to make him understand the cost. It wasn't just about the money, though that was clearly his immediate concern.

Hortense smiled at him. 'It's all right. I put some by most weeks. A few sous every time we sell a rabbit or get a good price for chickens in the market.'

Her husband got up slowly. 'I didn't know.' He got a chair and led her to it. 'Sit here for a bit. I'll get Monique.'

From her bedroom Hortense heard her eldest son come home. She heard him talking to his father, then the door closing. The house fell silent. François had taken the boys to the barn, plenty of stuff to mend out there.

The door opened and Joséphine came quietly into the room. She sat by her mother, holding her hand and from time to time wiping her face. 'Monique has gone for Mme Fachon, she won't be long. She's glad to do something away from the goats.'

As the latest contraction subsided, Hortense struggled to make sense of what her daughter had said. 'Who's glad to be away from the goats?'

'Monique.' Joséphine spoke in her usual blunt manner. 'Monique doesn't want to work here. She wants to be a *coiffeuse*. And she's worried that you'll die.'

'I'm not going to die.' Hortense reassured her daughter. 'Not long now and very soon you'll have a baby brother or sister. Thank you for looking after me. Run along now and make sure the little ones are fast asleep. Mme Fachon will be here soon.'

It was an odd situation for Hortense. The hours she was in labour were the only times when she was on her own and not working or looking after her family. She wondered how they would manage now that François no longer had a job. The idea that Monique wanted to leave home and become a hairdresser was something that had never entered her head. She considered her eldest daughter. What sort of life did she have? Fifteen years old and working long hours, day in day out, on the family smallholding. She could just about read and write. Between contractions it occurred to Hortense that her daughters might never marry, that all the young men were going away to war and even if they survived many would not come back to Forentan. But now was not the time to worry about how to deal with that problem.

She also realised that with no hope of work at Le Manoir

38

it was inevitable that Marcel would enlist. The thought of losing her boy filled her with dread.

What a world to bring a baby into.

Mme Angelique Fachon arrived with her bag. It was never quite clear what was in her bag, but it was clearly essential for a successful delivery. She had a good reputation and was in high demand in the villages around the area.

'Just as well you aren't a posh city lady.' Angelique Fachon busied herself with the contents of her mysterious bag.

'Is it?' Hortense was preoccupied with the increasing contractions and had no idea what the woman was talking about.

'They go to a lying-in hospital. If they've got the money that is. Nothing for people like me to do there.' It didn't occur to her that it might be possible for her to work in the hospital.

Just before midnight Gilbert Marie Durand made his way safely into the world. Angelique bound his robust little body in a linen cloth and gave him to her.

'I'll tell *Monsieur*.'

Hortense looked in wonder at her new son. She prayed for him, for his brothers and sisters and for the twins who died. She prayed for Marcel, she prayed for Monique and she prayed for François. She had no strength left to pray for herself. Exhausted, she closed her eyes and slept.

Forgive Me, Father

With only the briefest look at his wife, Gaston Lemonnier turned and strode out of his millinery shop. The last customer of the day, Mme Gaudin from Le Manoir, was waiting beside the road. Presumably someone would be along with a carriage to take her home. From habit he tipped his hat in her direction. The gesture was devoid of courtesy, there was no sense of deference. He did it because of custom, and a desire to get as much money as he could out of the old harridan.

Women, thought Gaston. The Lord is perfect and all-powerful, why did he create women? There would be time later that evening to consider this; he spent many evenings, and often a good part of many days, pondering the subject. The outcome was always the same, eventually he would resort to his cache of lewd photographs and pornographic magazines and the following day he'd go to confession with Père Dujardin. For the moment however he must put his negative thoughts about the female sex aside, there was business to attend to. He needed someone to work for him, a skivvy who would accept poor pay and not ask questions and he was on his way to see a likely candidate.

Long ago in the Lycée, the Revelations of St John the Divine had been drilled into the young Gaston by a succession of brothers. As a boy the prospect of eternal damnation had made him tremble; now tortured by his compulsion to look at images of depravity he feared for his soul in hell. He knew the agonies that awaited him. His pace slowed as he walked across the darkening square away from his shop, intoning under his breath the dreadful words from Revelations Chapter 21 that described his inevitable fate.

40

But the fearful, and unbelieving, and the abominable, and murderers, and whoremongers and sorcerers, and idolaters, and all liars, shall have their part in the lake which burns with fire and brimstone which is the second death.

He could see Christophe Pichon waiting by the dairy. He can bide his time, thought Lemonnier. The brothers had always made him wait. They used to make him wait to be let in, sometimes he had to shiver for hours in the cold, wait for the frequent chastisements and often wait for food. He was only told about his little sister's death from diphtheria three months after it happened. Let Pichon wait some more.

The brothers at Lycée Saint Aloysius had been welcoming at first. Seven-year-old Gaston had settled in well; he was a bright child and keen to learn. His father had plans for him to be a lawyer, but these had to be forgotten when Lemonnier père was jailed in 1876 for embezzlement. But things had already started to go wrong for young Gaston. When he was ten years old a change in the governance of the Lycée heralded a shift in the attitude towards the boys. Abuse and neglect became commonplace; his family were probably unaware of his situation. He didn't see them for five years as their circumstances spiralled downwards following his father's implication in a series of fraudulent transactions.

It had occurred to Lemonnier that employing the youth might create more problems than it solved. Women again. He'd heard that Pichon's girl was pregnant. The thought of human procreation filled him with disgust. He pictured the Garden of Eden, unsullied and glorious until it was defiled by Eve. Dragging his mind back to Pichon, he realised that the advantage of having a man with responsibilities meant that he could have a tighter control over what he did, the hours he worked and what he was paid.

'So, Pichon, you have kept our appointment.'

'*Oui,* Monsieur, I understand you would like me to work for you.'

'Yes, this is for regular work. You have done some casual work for me; now I would like you to work for me every day.'

Gaston Lemonnier enjoyed watching the lad squirm. He held all the cards; there was no room for negotiation. Christophe needed regular work with pay, especially if he was going to marry that whore Odille, and there was no other work available. He might join the army, but in Gaston's opinion he wouldn't be much use as a soldier with that injured foot. With a smirk the milliner recalled the occasion when he'd asked Christophe to collect a parcel for him. The stupid boy had asked him what was in it! He'd been tempted to show him some of the pornography, but instead accused him of spying for Mme Lemonnier. A much better tactic as it let him keep the moral high ground, and in his eyes it gave him an additional reason to keep the wages low.

He watched Christophe turn away and then hesitate before turning to accept the job. Lemonnier knew he would, in spite of the pittance he was being offered and the hours he would have to work. The milliner had his *bon à tout faire*.

'Start tomorrow.' It wasn't a question.

'What time?'

'6.30, don't be late.'

Gaston walked away from the dairy across the square towards the *tabac*. Bernard Lavoisier had a package for him; he'd seen the carrier arrive that morning. He hesitated. Did he have the strength to burn the package unopened as

42

he'd promised the priest? No, he didn't. It was Christine's fault. He knew his wife was ill. It was obvious. She had always been scrawny, but she'd become skeletal. Why didn't the stupid woman say something? What had she done to cause the illness? The Lord was omnipotent so Gaston determined that he would pray that He would prevail upon Christine to tell him the truth.

The conception of their daughter following their marriage had been a source of embarrassment and misery for both Gaston and Christine. Once the deed was done they retreated permanently to separate bedrooms. For a while Gaston couldn't even look at his erotica, such was his horror.

When Amelie was born he thought he'd be disappointed; he badly wanted a son and he realised that there weren't going to be any more pregnancies in his marriage. But the little girl was beautiful; he hadn't felt love for another human being for many years. He named her Amelie after his little sister, because both of them had sweet smiles and nice natures. Here was female perfection, untainted by venal thoughts and physical impurities.

And God shall wipe away all tears from their eyes; and there shall be no more death, neither sorrow, nor crying, neither shall there be any more pain.

But the miracle came to an abrupt end in September 1908. Most years there were epidemics of one sort or another. Polio, diphtheria, cholera, smallpox and typhoid were common, and children were the most vulnerable. This year summer was drawing to an end, the days were cooler and it seemed that for once Forentan had escaped an outbreak of disease. But a late polio epidemic that autumn was virulent, claiming many lives. Gaston tried everything

43

to save his daughter, bringing in a physician from Louche-la-Mustique to treat her. Amelie did live, but she never walked again.

The milliner got to the *tabac* just as Lavoisier was clearing up the mess left behind by the drunken antics of the Fischers. It seemed to Gaston that there was no point in serving them. They drove away any other customers. Who could enjoy a drink or meet a friend when those two were fighting at the next table? The milliner concluded, rightly, that there was more to the relationship between Bernard and Marie-Pierre Fischer than he knew about. Why else would the man put up with such behaviour in his café?

Lavoisier handed him the tattered package; it was obvious that it had been opened and carelessly reassembled. At first Gaston was angry, and ashamed that his predilections were now in the public domain. He was unaware that they already were. His wife, the soon-to-be-wife of Christophe Pichon, a lad called Marcel who shot pigeons with a catapult and, of course, the priest, and now Bernard all knew about his stash of pornography. Up until now this disparate group of people had had their reasons for keeping quiet about this, but times and attitudes were changing. This was something Gaston had not yet realised.

As he walked home with his package Gaston wondered about Amelie. As far as he could tell, her mother was dying. Who would look after the girl? She needed constant attention; Gaston recoiled at the thought of what this must involve. He would need help, but he couldn't countenance the prospect of anyone else living in the *appartement* above the shop. It was necessary to talk to Christine. Find out what was wrong with her, and then decide what to do about Amelie.

Forgive me, Father, for I have sinned.
The package in his hands grew heavier with every step
he took.

Secrets and Lies

I really don't know what else I could've done. I hope no one finds out. With a bit of luck and some hard work on my back for a couple of weeks it'll be OK. I did wonder if anyone would believe me when I let little bits of my 'secret' out. I couldn't have been more wrong, they all jumped at the possibility of a bit of scandal. Most of the people in this town haven't got anything else to interest them. What really clinched it was me telling miserable old Mme Lemonnier. Her face! She looked like she was chewing a wasp. Anyway, she told me that I was worse than a whore and that she wouldn't be needing my services anymore.

If I really was in the family way then I wouldn't say anything, would I? I'd get myself off to see Madame Solange in the Rue des Anges and get everything sorted out. When I told Christophe the good news he was really surprised. I told him that kissing with tongues is what did it. Anyway, he's such a poppet he didn't argue – just said he'd get some work and we'd be married.

My friend Claudine said they don't take married men into the army, so if I can marry him before the recruiting officer comes, he won't have to go. I know he wants to join up; him and that Marcel Durand have been planning it for weeks. They think it'll be a laugh and that they'll get free boots and a good meal every day. I told Christophe that it's not all fun and games. My mum said that her uncle Rudolphe was in the battle at Sedan. He came home with only one leg and a wound in his throat where a bullet went right through. Every time he tried to eat the food just came straight out of the hole.

The one I feel sorry for is that poor kid Amelie. Stuck up there in that horrible room, day in day out, with her sour old mother and weird father. The other day I found him reading something and he didn't half go for me. Accused me of spying on him. Filthy old goat, I know what he gets up to. If I tell you something, you'll keep it a secret, won't you? Don't breathe a word of this. When Claudine was about twelve, old Lemonnier asked her to do something special for him. She went to his office at the back of his shop. It was horrible, too horrible for her to tell me. He had one of these new cameras that anyone can use and he kept taking photographs of her doing bad things.

She was ever so upset and she told her sister what had happened. Her sister told their mum and Claudine got into a lot of trouble. Her mother washed her mouth out with carbolic soap every day for a week, didn't give her any food for four days and then gave her a good beating with a butter paddle. Apparently she was evil to think such things. The worst bit is that her sister, the one she told about it all, got *le diphthérie* and died a month after all this happened. Their mum said it was all Claudine's fault and that her sister's throat had closed over, even though they treated her with *Violet de Paris*, because she'd said dreadful words.

Anyway, poor little Amelie has got a crush on Christophe. She told me. Well she hasn't got anyone else to talk to. She watches the square in the hope of seeing him. She gets really down when she doesn't see him for a few days. Poor little cow. She'll be devastated when she finds out we're getting married.

Thinking about it, I wonder if moody Christine Lemonnier is alright? She's got ever so thin lately and she sort of holds her side and walks funny. Wouldn't surprise me if she had some illness or other. On the other hand it might be just because she's sad, living with that pervert and a sick daughter.

Who's that man in a scruffy cart? Looks like some sort

of photographer. The horse is just a few steps from the knacker's yard, that's for sure. He's been round the square twice. Hoping for business I guess. He won't get much here, everyone's skint – though I suppose he could take my wedding photograph. That would be one in the eye for Christine Lemonnier. I would need some money though; I wonder how much he charges?

Money is my biggest problem, well lack of it to be accurate. I haven't got a *sou* to my name. For a start we'll need somewhere to live. Aunt Berthe has told me that I'm no longer welcome in her house. Miserable woman. My mum did a lot for her, helped her in all sorts of ways when Uncle Jerome pushed off. I suppose she did take me in when Mum died, but I've done my bit. I bring in a few francs a week looking after Amelie, and I do all the laundry for her. She says she's ashamed of me. Who's she to talk! She couldn't keep her husband – he left her for a widow who only had one leg.

We'll have to see if we can get a room in the *logement* where the Fischers live. It's very run down, and alive with cockroaches, but then beggars can't be choosers. It'll only be for a bit until we can afford somewhere better. It all hinges on Christophe getting a job. He told me he'd got something in mind, but he wouldn't say what it was.

Christophe will tell me tonight if he's been successful. Then we'll have to go and see Père Dujardin. I expect he knows my 'secret'. I made sure his nosey housekeeper was close enough to hear when I was talking to Claudine in the bakery yesterday. She'll tell the priest and he'll do the business. Fancy me being married!

I hope Claudine is right about them not taking married men into the army. Sometimes she just makes things up and believes they're true. The trouble is there's a war on, and they seem to think that more men will have to go to fight. I don't want Christophe to go away; he might not want to come back when he's seen how exciting being in the army is. He doesn't listen to me telling him he might get hurt or even killed. And he might meet some of those city girls and forget all about Odille in Forentan. I've got to find someone to marry, there's nothing here for girls who aren't married. I'll end up on the game if I don't find someone soon and if I'm not quick about it all the men will have gone away. And Christophe is *mignon*, I've just got to keep him. No, I've done the right thing, the only thing, just got to get a baby going as quickly as possible when we are married.

I'm keeping well out of the way this evening, no one knows I'm here, tucked away in a corner beside the town hall. I want to keep an eye on Christophe and see if he really is trying to get a job. If he gets a good job he might give up the idea of joining the army. We'll still get married though; I'd like to be Madame Pichon.

Who's this coming up the street? *Mon dieu* it's only Marcel with his mum and some of his endless brothers and sisters. Those Durands are like rabbits, they have a new one every year and by the look of her it's only a matter of days before she has the next one. I've got to hand it to her, she somehow keeps them all clothed and they get enough to eat. That doesn't stop Marcel wanting to get away. I don't blame him, there's nothing here for him, but I don't want him taking his mate Christophe as well.

Now, what's happening with the Fischers? Every evening they get drunk and have an argument. Seems like they're having a right old barney tonight. Ouch, that'll hurt. That woman has got some strength. Even with a skinful of absinthe she can wallop a chair over his head. I reckon old Bernard is sweet on her and that's why she gets so many drinks every evening.

49

Who's that Christophe is talking to? Oh, not creepy Lemonnier. *Merde*. I know I said any sort of job, but with him! It won't pay very much, but anything is better than nothing I suppose.

Fly on the Wall

It was getting dark as Gilles Poussin arrived in the centre of Forentan. He looked sadly at his tired horse. Poor Hirondelle, he mused, she won't last another winter on these roads, and I don't know what I'll do then. The cart, pulled so slowly and with such difficulty by the old horse, drew mostly ridicule these days. Fourteen years ago it had been a different story. *Gilles Poussin: Premier Artiste Photographique du Monde* had glowed in brilliant gold and blue on both sides of the cart. Hirondelle, glossy and sprightly, trotted joyfully from village to town, through cities and hamlets, and everywhere people wanted to have their photograph taken. Young and old stood, severe and proud, while Poussin fussed and fiddled: an alchemist at the very beginning of the 20th Century, immortalising ordinary people and making gods of the well-to-do.

Now very few people even bothered to look at him. In most towns these days there was a photographic studio and his business of travelling picture-taker was like his horse, clearly on its last legs. Quite a few people these days even had their own Kodak Brownie cameras. Moving pictures were the business to be in. Only last month he had been to see *L'Affaire d'Orcival*; the cinema was packed.

Poussin looked around the Place de la République; he saw nothing that made him think this town would be any different to all the other places he had stopped at over the last couple of years. Every town he visited looked poor and dilapidated, the inhabitants malnourished and dispirited. He recalled that he had been to Forentan before, about eight years previously. The many places he had visited got mixed up in his memory, but something about this place made him think of a pretty child with miserable parents. They had been good customers and their purchases had encouraged others. In the morning he'd see if his memory was playing tricks. He wished he had a

51

moving picture camera that he could use to capture these people, immortalise them in celluloid. He had investigated the equipment he would need to make cine film. It was heavy and cumbersome, but he already had ideas about how he could modify it to make it lighter and easier to move and use. It was also expensive, and Gilles was down to his last few francs.

Hirondelle plodded in the direction of the Rue des Anges where Gilles knew there were cheap lodgings and stables. And women, if you wanted one, but Poussin had neither the money, nor these days even the inclination, for that. He looked at his watch, it was 6.35. Maybe he'd have enough money for a beer if he paid for his board and lodging, and the stable, up-front. As the cart lurched across the square he saw the name above the milliner's shop. Lemonnier! That was it, the sour man with the pretty daughter. He'd taken some good photographs of the little girl dancing; perhaps they'd be keen to have some new ones. Outside the *tabac* he saw a couple drinking. Silent and remote they stared into the distance, pausing only to call for a refill as the shabby cart trundled past their table.

By the dairy a young man was shifting from foot to foot. Poussin wondered what he was doing; it looked as if he was either waiting for someone or up to mischief. Hirondelle stumbled, abruptly ending the photographer's musings. He gave the youth no further consideration, concentrating on safely negotiating the last few yards. Out of the corner of his eye he noticed something, or someone, moving in the fading light. With eyes accustomed to noticing details he saw a young woman hide behind the crumbling columns that marked the entrance to the town hall. What's she up to? Probably a tart he decided. He didn't for one moment imagine that she might be a potential customer for him.

Passing the church he saw a glimmer of light reflected on one of the windows. Who's praying at this hour he wondered. *Thank God I'm not the only sinner.* There were quite a few people about, some shopping, others passing the

52

time and in some cases drinking. *If I could take a picture of them all*, he said to himself, *then I'd have enough money for a bed that wasn't full of fleas and Hirondelle wouldn't have to share her stable with so many rats.*

If it hadn't been for that indiscretion with the baker's wife in Louche-la-Mustique he would have had enough money to have his own premises. He might have even been able to buy the cine camera he craved so much. In any case he'd be comfortably off by now, not scraping a mere existence travelling in all weathers in a clapped-out horse and cart. All sorts of people seemed to have an automobile these days. Only last week he'd seen the bishop being driven around in a very smart De Dion Bouton. Gilles wanted one just like that.

The war with Germany was already making a difference to France, even in the remote rural areas. On the one hand the atmosphere of jingoistic euphoria that had characterised the onset of war in August had worn off, and people were increasingly worried and uncertain. But on the other hand there was also a demand for photographs of sons and husbands, smart and handsome in uniform, ready to go and fight the *Boche*. The problem was that these portraits were usually done in a studio, not in a makeshift tent on the back of an old cart. The world was changing and Gilles knew it was the end for his travelling photography enterprise. Films were being made of the war, mostly rather boring propaganda films, but he sensed that the war provided him with an opportunity.

There was talk of the formation of a military film department. Apparently there was a lot of footage being shot and no one seemed to know what to do with it. Gilles reasoned that if he enlisted and made a lot of his knowledge of photography and cinematographic equipment he stood a good chance of getting into this section. The more he thought about it the better it sounded. He would enlist and do his patriotic duty without actually fighting. At forty-nine and with a gammy leg, caused many years ago by a kick from Hirondelle when he was training her to pull the cart, he surmised that he wouldn't be any good on the front line. But he had expertise with cameras and film, and that's what was needed.

By 7.30 it was dark. He had sorted out his horse and arranged for food and a bed for himself. 'These October nights draw in so fast,' he grumbled to the slovenly landlord who showed him to the room he was to share with three others.

'Happens every year,' responded the other and made his way to the kitchen, wiping his hands on his grimy apron as he shuffled through the door.

As he ate his meal, Poussin wondered about the people in the town he had just seen: those he had photographed eight years earlier and those he had just seen who had their own stories to tell. He remembered the girl by the town hall. Was she a prostitute touting for business? If so why did she hide? He asked the questions he had asked so many times before; how can I really know what they are doing? If only I could be a fly on the wall. As he chewed on his gristly meat he embellished his plan. With a cine camera he could film ordinary people going about their daily business. He would be a sensation. His mind was made up. He would join up, get into cinematography and when the war was over leave the army and be part of the future, not holding onto the past.

PART 2

1924

News from a Small Town

Gilles Poussin manoeuvred the Renault van, loaded with all his cinematographic equipment, into the old stable. He could not recall if it was the same stable where he'd left his horse Hirondelle all those years ago, but it looked like it. In those days the stables had been full of horses, people and rats. Now they stood forlorn and empty. They could turn these into proper garages. He left his van and made his way into the hotel. The place had changed for the better over the last ten years; when he stayed here before the food had made him ill, now it was clean and well kept. The sullen and slovenly landlord he remembered had morphed into a ruthlessly efficient woman with a bun and a pince-nez.

Forentan had not changed very much from the sleepy little town that he remembered. The church looked even more dilapidated, the roof sagged badly and the stonework around the door was loose; he could see chunks of mortar lying beside the main door. Ragged children were everywhere, in fact there were probably more than the last time he had been here. The shops were much the same, though he noticed that the milliners had become a general drapery shop and the run-down *tabac* on the opposite side of the square was now a busy restaurant. He'd been told that the *cassoulet* there was sublime; he looked forward to his lunch the next day with anticipation.

Gilles had spent the war as an army photographer. His attempts to portray the brutality of what he had witnessed had been largely frustrated by a military machine that only wanted to show success and glory. But as hostilities shuddered to a conclusion in 1918 he was able to circulate a more accurate description of what was going on. For Gilles the best outcome was being able to use cinematography. Finally he had been able to film the reality of shell-shock, of gas gangrene and of the appalling conditions that soldiers endured in the trenches. It had not been easy, he still had flashbacks and the smell of chlorine made him sick.

Now he was working for Pathé News, and his assignment this time was to look at how rural and small-town France had changed since 1920. When he was given the job he had encountered considerable opposition. His bosses wanted him to portray a resurgent France, not only coping with the aftermath of war, but surging ahead. Gilles knew this was not the case; fortunately one of the directors backed him. Once he had approval Gilles thought straight away of Forentan, a small town, off the beaten track and far from the eyes of the world. And he had some unfinished business in Forentan; he wanted to get this out of the way before he got immersed in filming. As soon as he had sorted out his accommodation he went to the bakery to make enquiries; everyone bought bread on at least a daily basis. As he entered the shop the baker Joubert stopped sweeping crumbs from a shelf behind the counter and greeted the stranger with a cautious '*Bonjour, Monsieur.*'

Gilles came straight to the point. '*Bonjour, Monsieur.* Perhaps you can help me. I am looking for someone. A lady called Mme Odille Pichon.'

Louis Joubert narrowed his eyes as he scrutinised Gilles. 'Who wants to know?'

'My name is Gilles Poussin, I work for Pathé News.'

'No one round here called that.' Joubert sounded unconvincing.

'I have something for her. If you are able to get a message to that lady, please ask her to meet me. With your permission I will meet her here, in your presence so that you can see my business is honourable.'

'I'll see what I can do. Come back this evening at 6.00. I'll be here.'

Gilles spent a useful day walking around the town, making notes and taking photographs. There was certainly enough

57

material here for the newsreel he was planning. In the morning market he had seen a young man clearly suffering from shell-shock. The symptoms were immediately recognisable to him: the intense stare into the distance, the involuntary shaking and the occasional hideous scream. Gilles had also noted that, as in everywhere he went, women far outnumbered men. Only boys, a few weedy adolescents, old men and those damaged by conflict remained.

There were some positive changes. People seemed a bit more open, not exactly welcoming, as his conversation with the baker had shown, but less aggressive towards him than they had been when he had trundled into the town a decade earlier with his horse-drawn photographic studio. And there was the restaurant! What a meal he enjoyed there. It had been transformed from a seedy bar to somewhere worth travelling along those awful roads to get to.

Tomorrow he'd make a start. Gilles decided to give his newsreel 'News from a Small Town' as a working title. He would show the world what was happening in Forentan, depicting the town as a microcosm of France in 1924. It seemed to him that everything about France came from Paris and other major cities. Gilles saw it as his mission to show what was happening in the more remote parts of this diverse country to the wider world.

He had another reason to come to Forentan. In his valise he had a small packet, carefully wrapped in brown paper. At 5.30 exactly he went to his room, opened his case and retrieved the packet. It was almost unbelievable that he had kept it for all these years, and a miracle that it had survived. But it had, and he was now on the brink of delivering it. He wondered if he'd be offered some money for it, but he didn't want that any more. He deeply regretted insisting on a few francs all those years ago; he was here to make amends.

At 6.00 he was outside the bakery. A woman came towards him from the direction of the church. Was she familiar? There was only one way to find out. He removed his cap and inclined his head. 'Madame Pichon?'

Giles sat up late that evening, smoking cigarettes and drinking indifferent wine in the bar of his hotel. He was the only guest, and the concierge with a bun made it very clear that she wanted him to go to his room so that she could lock up. But he didn't want to go to bed; his meeting with Odille Pichon had unsettled him. He should have been more sensitive, he should not have just given her the photograph, and he should have prepared her for what was in the packet that he handed to her. It had never occurred to him that this would be the first time that Odille had ever seen a photograph of her husband, the first time in years that she had seen his features. Seeing the anguish in her beautiful face when she saw the image of the man she loved taught Gilles a lot about his responsibility as a photographer. He had wanted to put his arm around her and comfort her, but all he could do was pretend to look at something in his bag while she struggled to bring her emotions under control.

She wanted to pay him; embarrassed, he looked at the ground. '*Pas nécessaire*' was all he could say. How he wished that he hadn't refused to give her the photograph ten years ago. For the sake of a few francs! How he wanted to turn the clock back.

Gilles spent the next week working on his film. He liked to do as much of the work as possible himself, but if he needed help there were always lads to give him a hand in exchange for a few francs. He became well known in the town, especially by the youngsters who did all they could to get into the range of the camera shots. Some of the older people refused to be filmed, though he did take some surreptitious footage of them. He was mindful of the effect that seeing the photograph had had on Odille Pichon and he selected his shots carefully. But mostly people were happy to be filmed going about their daily business.

He wanted to include Marcel Durand in his footage, showing how the ravages of war continued to take their toll even in out-of-the-way settlements like Forentan. Once he would have just filmed the man, cowering and screaming, hiding behind his mother. He decided to talk to Mme Durand, explain what he wanted to do and try to get her cooperation. He did not relish the prospect. In the event the conversation with Hortense Durand was less difficult than he imagined. She wanted the world to know about men like her son; she had no idea that thousands of others were suffering in the same way as him. Gilles filmed Marcel in the market far enough away so that he and his mother could not be recognised but close enough for the terror and anguish of shell-shock to be obvious to anyone who saw the film. He never regretted not taking the opportunity of a close-up of Marcel's tormented face. Other film makers were less circumspect.

The situation with Mme Odille Pichon was more problematic. It was rapidly becoming obvious to Gilles that he was attracted to this woman, and he did not know what to do. He had experience with many women; he had had a reputation as a lothario in his younger days. His conquests had included single women and married women, but never as far as he could recall, a widow, and a war widow at that. In addition he realised that his feelings for Odille were not simply physical; he admired her determination and her ambition for her daughter, and he respected the love that she clearly still had for her dead husband. He had no idea what to do.

The footage he had taken of Forentan was complete. It was time for him to go back to the studio in Paris and begin the task of editing. He had heard that Odille Pichon was losing her job as housekeeper for the priest. This might make it difficult to see her without causing gossip. He slowly packed his few belongings, wondering how soon he could contrive to re-visit Forentan and see Odille without upsetting the sensitivities of the town.

There was a knock on his door. He opened it to find Mme Pince-Nez visibly bristling with righteous indignation. 'Monsieur Poussin, this is unacceptable. This is a respectable hotel.'

'Madame, I am confused. What is wrong?'

The concierge sniffed virtuously.

'Downstairs.' She rolled her eyes. 'Downstairs. The widow Pichon. She is asking to see you.'

The Likeness of Christophe Pichon

Mère Agnès was worried. The responsibilities of the convent weighed heavily on her slight shoulders. Although she had other nuns to help with the day-to-day running of the convent the final decisions and accountability lay with her. Mère Agnès was by nature a pragmatic woman, not worrying unduly at the first signs of a problem but, when the inevitable daily niggles escalated into real difficulties she frequently wished that she had not accepted the post of Mother Superior.

The cause for her latest concern was not even one of the nuns. It was a young woman, crippled by polio, who had lived in the convent for ten years. Amelie had arrived as a frightened, angry, child. Slowly she had settled down and over the years had become an important part of the community, inspiring novices and older nuns with her fortitude and resilience. More importantly, in Mère Agnès' eyes, she had brought money and prestige to this small and remote convent. Amelie was a skilled and inspired needlewoman. Not only had she embroidered chasubles and orfreys that were in high demand throughout the diocese and beyond, but she also had the skill and patience to teach others. As a result the convent was now regarded as a centre of excellence for needlework and attracted plenty of able novices along with generous endowments from their families.

'You need to decide.' Mère Agnès was once again trying to find out why Amelie consistently refused to become a novice.

'*Mère*, I cannot make this decision now. With your permission I would like to leave the convent on a temporary basis. I need to see what is outside these walls before I can decide to stay within them.'

'*Ma fille, ce n'est pas possible.* Here you have Sisters

62

to care for you, attend to your physical needs and value your contribution to our Lord. Beyond these walls there is no one to care for you, no one to turn to.'

'I have a little money. I will use that to pay for a maid to care for me.'

Mère Agnès considered this suggestion carefully. She wondered if by allowing Amelie to leave the convent for a while she might resolve the problem. The older woman knew enough of the world to understand how difficult it was for a young woman, confined to a wheelchair, without a family, and as far as she could see no possibility of finding a husband, to be able to live on her own. She discussed the matter with Sister Sybille, the convent's treasurer and her long-time friend and confidante.

'Let her go.' Sister Sybille was unequivocal. 'Let her go. She'll be back in no time. If she still won't take her vows, then we'll find another role for her. She's too important to lose.' The treasurer knew better than anyone how much the convent relied on the income from Amelie's embroidery.

Fortified by her friend's confidence Mère Agnès made some arrangements. First she wrote to her brother. Henri Cotrel was a curator of Egyptian antiquities at the Louvre in Paris and through his contacts she secured temporary employment for Amelie assisting in the conservation of ecclesiastical vestments. It surprised her to learn that the skill of her protégé was recognised even in the Louvre. She had always taken Amelie's ability seriously, but now it was clear just how good she was.

'Where can she live in Paris?' Henri had been unable to help his sister solve this problem. A convent seemed the obvious answer, but Mère Agnès had other ideas.

'If she goes to a convent in Paris they'll keep her! We'll

never see her again in Louche-la-Mustique,' she confided to Sister Sybille.

'And she won't properly see the world beyond the convent walls.' Sister Sybille didn't want Amelie to find life easy in Paris. 'No, she needs to live as independently as possible. Find out just how tough it is.'

A fortnight before Amelie was due to leave for Paris, Mère Agnès found her in the chapel, her wheelchair directly in front of the wall hanging she had completed about eighteen months after she came to live in the convent. The embroidery depicted St Christophe carrying the Christ Child over a raging river. The image showed skill and maturity beyond the years of the teenager who had created it.

'Of all your work, this gives you the greatest pleasure *n'est-ce pas*?'

Amelie turned towards the Mother Superior. 'It means a lot to me, yes.'

'Well, you'll have to live without it. I have found an apartment for you in Paris.'

She saw the profound effect that her words had on Amelie. She sensed the apprehension and fear in her young charge. She probably hasn't thought through all the implications of leaving the convent, Mère Agnès surmised to herself. Out loud she said, 'You can change your mind, stay here, take your vows.

'No, I cannot do that. I will go. Thank you for arranging this for me.' Amelie laboriously turned her chair round to take her leave.

'You have not been dismissed.'

Amelie obediently manoeuvred her cumbersome chair to face Mère Agnès.

'You must tell me why you are so reluctant to take your vows.' As she spoke she realised that she knew the answer to the question that she'd struggled with for so long. This understanding struck the elderly nun with the force of a blow. 'It's that wall hanging, isn't it? That is you being carried across the storms of life to safety.' As she spoke she was aware of the young woman crumpling in her high-backed chair. Amelie quickly pulled herself together.

'*C'est vrai.*' Her voice stayed calm, but so soft it sounded like snow falling onto winter trees. 'Yes, it is me, and the Christ bearer is a man also called Christophe. I loved him. He is dead now, he died at Passchendaele. But I had already lost him. He married in 1914.'

'So this brave young man is the reason why you cannot take your vows. Surely you...' Mère Agnès did not have the words to voice her concern that a crippled young woman, scarcely more than a child when she came to the convent, could have had any sort of intimate relationship.

'No, Mother, I loved him from afar. I could never be close to him, even to speak to him. He would not have even been aware of my feelings.'

Mère Agnès resisted the temptation to say that it was time that Amelie got over this infatuation. It wasn't love; love is reciprocal. But the pain etched on the young woman's face stopped her. Instead she said, 'Thank you for your honesty. You need to reflect on the love that our heavenly father has for you and come back to me when you have considered this. Meanwhile I wish you well in Paris. I have asked Sister Monique to accompany you; she will attend to you for six months. Then she will return to Louche-la-Mustique. If you decide to stay in Paris you must make your own arrangements.'

That evening when compline had ended and the nuns were making their way back to their cells, Mère Agnès remained in the chapel. She took a seat in front of the image of St

65

Christophe, holding her lantern high enough to be able to see the face of the carrier of the Christ Child. She moved slightly so that she could also inspect the face of the child. Now she knew that this was modelled on Amelie and the Saint inspired by another bearer of the name Christophe, she reflected on the nature of love. She had known the love of her family until she became a novice, when earthly love was superseded by the love of the Heavenly Father, whom she loved with every fibre of her being. The love that Amelie had felt, indeed still felt, for Christophe was something she could not fully comprehend. But now, late in her life she was beginning to recognise the validity of love in its diverse manifestations. By the flickering light of the guttering candle she prayed for the soul of the young man who had died in the trenches and she prayed for Amelie, willing her to commit herself to God. Her prayer finished, she crossed herself, rose and with a sigh made her way carefully out of the darkening chapel towards her cell.

The Legacy of War

Gilbert Durand ran excitedly into the kitchen. '*Douze oeufs, Maman, douze oeufs!*'

Hortense carefully inspected and admired the basket of eggs proffered by her youngest son. '*Merveilleux*, put them in the pantry please. Be careful; we don't want any cracks today. I'll have a nice lot to take to the market tomorrow.' Hortense Durand's eyes switched from the exuberance of the boy to the figure of her eldest son. Marcel had enlisted in 1914 looking for adventure and a bright future. Instead he experienced the horrors of the front line, fighting not only the enemy but also the hellish conditions of the trenches. Unlike so many others, including his pal Christophe Pichon, Marcel had returned to Forentan in 1918 a broken man both mentally and physically. Today his mother could see him in the orchard, hiding behind the apple tree he used to climb when he was Gilbert's age. Being in the orchard gave him some peace, but not for long. Any unexpected sound would cause him to scream, pull his coat over his head and shake with uncontrollable tremors. Hortense had no idea how to help him.

Trying to comfort Marcel was not her only concern that morning. She looked again at the letter that had arrived the previous day. It was from her eldest daughter. Monique had joined the convent at Louche-la-Mustique seven years ago and taken her vows. This had been a great relief to her parents. Prospects for poor country girls were limited, and following the carnage of the war there were now very few young men to provide enough husbands. Hortense and her husband François had travelled to Louche-la-Mustique to see their daughter take her vows. It was a proud moment for them and the twenty-five kilometres to and from the town was the furthest either of them had ever travelled. It was also the last time that Monique would see her father; he died in the influenza epidemic of 1919 leaving her mother to raise their children, and care for Marcel.

'Dear Maman, I hope that you are well and that the kids are all behaving themselves.' *No mention of Marcel, thought Hortense, and doesn't she realise they aren't babies anymore?* But these niggles were quickly forgotten. The rest of the letter left her stunned and feeling more bereft than she had felt since the day François died.

'*Maman*, come quickly. Marcel is shouting.' It was her second daughter calling to her from the back yard. Joséphine was slow to learn and had to do things very methodically, but she was a considerable help as long as she didn't have to hurry.

Later, when Marcel was calm and she'd washed and put salve over a bad graze on Gilbert's knee, caused when he tripped while trying to jump over a churn, she returned to Monique's letter. The daughter that she was so proud of was renouncing her vows. She was leaving the convent, and in Hortense's eyes, walking away from God. Worse was to come. It appeared that she had been sent to Paris for six months by her Mother Superior. Her task had been to attend to Amelie Lemonnier who was working in the Louvre. Hortense knew Amelie; she was a Forentan girl crippled by polio. She had gone to live in the convent when her dying mother could no longer care for her. Hortense crossed herself when she thought about Amelie's late father. He had died more than six years ago, and she did not want to think ill of the dead, but she had heard that he had had some disgraceful habits and had been accustomed to doing bad things in the privacy of his office. She had no idea what this could possibly have been. She had led a sheltered life, but enough people had told her how disgusting he had been to cause her to recoil at the mention of his name.

The letter told her that while in Paris, Monique had met a man and fallen in love. Worse was to come. The man in question was not only a journalist but he was also English. *Quel horreur!* Hortense read the rest of the letter with a growing sense of disbelief. This could not be true. Her daughter had renounced her vows and was planning to marry this man and go to live in London.

Sleep for Hortense was impossible that night. She rose at 5.30 and loaded her handcart with eggs, a crate of live chickens, some vegetables from the garden and four rabbits. She killed the rabbits and hung them by their back legs from a bar fixed above the handcart. Marcel was awake; he rarely slept. Hortense asked him to push the cart; it gave him something to do and if he was with her at least she knew he was safe. She didn't think it fair to his siblings for them to have to deal with his outbursts. Although in town boys taunted him and people she considered should know better stared at him and muttered '*Imbecile*', dealing with that was preferable to leaving him at home.

It wasn't far into the centre of town, and by 7.00 she was ready to start selling. She had a good morning, trade was brisk and Marcel seemed almost relaxed. She encouraged him to eat a small piece of bread and someone from another stall gave him a slice of melon.

At noon everyone began to clear up and make their way home for the midday meal. Hortense went to see her old friend, the baker Louis Joubert. Over the years they had helped each other, and both had been widowed within a few days by the same flu epidemic. Now Louis's son ran the boulangerie, but Joubert *père* was usually in the shop serving the customers.

'Can I speak to you in private?' The queue at midday was always long.

'Maud, come here and serve. Now, *s'il te plait*.' Louis's

69

granddaughter emerged reluctantly from the back room. 'I won't be long. Remember to smile for the customers. What's wrong, Hortense?'

She showed him the letter from Monique. He read it slowly then handed it back to her. 'There is nothing you can do. That is what makes it difficult. We want the best for our children, but their paths take them in ways we cannot possibly imagine.' He glanced across at Marcel. 'You can pray that this man, this Englishman, is a good man but I think that is all you can do.'

'But he might be a Protestant. I've got to do something.' Hortense twisted her market apron into a knot. Inside the shop the queue was growing restless, Maud was slow and everyone wanted to get home for their meal. Louis patted her hand. 'I must go now. Would you permit me to visit you this afternoon when the shop is closed? We can talk about this some more.'

Hortense was unsure; she didn't want tongues to wag but reasoned she had nothing to lose and she needed to talk this through with her trusted friend. 'That would be very useful. *À tout à l'heure.*'

She turned to leave and saw that Odille Pichon was in the queue with her daughter Jeanne-Christophe. *That child is the image of her father*, thought Hortense. Christophe Pichon had died at Passchendaele; Marcel had survived to return to Forentan but she sadly reflected that it might have been better if he had died alongside his friend. Putting this dreadful thought aside she realised that Odille Pichon was talking to Marcel.

'Say hello to M Pichon,' Odille instructed her daughter.

'*Bonjour, Monsieur Pichon,*' the little girl dutifully mumbled.

'*Oncle Marcel.*' He said his name clearly, Hortense felt a shock run through her body. Only two words but it proved he could speak normally.

70

The little girl was telling Marcel about a kitten that Père Michel had given her. He seemed soothed by her chattering; he did not take his eyes away from her animated face. Hortense wondered if he recognised the image of his lost friend in Christophe's daughter.

The queue moved and the Durands began their walk home with an almost empty handcart. 'I hope Joséphine has prepared our lunch. What do you think it will be?' Hortense tried to engage her son but he had lost the rapport he had had with Christophe's child.

They were almost home and one of the dogs came dancing down the track to meet them. As Marcel bent down to greet the dog, his attention was taken by something almost hidden in the long grass between the track and a field. It glinted in the midday sun, a roll of fencing wire to keep the goats out of the vegetable garden, a job that his father had not lived long enough to complete. His screams tore the air. The terrified dog ran back to the house, Joséphine and Gilbert dashed out to find out what was wrong. Hortense tried helplessly and hopelessly to calm him. All she could hear through the dreadful screams were the words

'Fil barbelé! Fil barbelé! Attention fil barbelé!'

Déjeuner Chez Bernard

Georges Hibou was enjoying his meal, savouring the tasty sausages and adding a small amount of his wine to the gravy so that the last morsel of bread soaked up the delicious juice. He planned to allow his lunch to settle; perhaps a small *digestif* would help that, before he walked around Forentan to make sure all was well. He did not intend to spend much time in the Rue des Anges. Who knew what can of worms he might disturb if he poked his nose in there? The brothel, the sweatshops, the printer with a sideline in imitation bank notes, and the makers of counterfeit goods were all known to Georges, but it never occurred to him to do anything about them. Realistically he stood no chance of closing them down even if he did try. Too much money was being paid to men in high places to make it worth any gendarme risking his job, and his neck, to probe into their activities.

He noticed the *patronne*, Marie-Pierre Lavoisier, peeping at him from the small front window of the bistro. It had surprised him how busy Chez Bernard was, serving as many people as could be seated in the tiny dining room and on the pavement outside. The plat du jour, the *cassoulet*, that he had enjoyed so much was popular and as it was a mild day some customers had opted for the *charcuterie*. Georges briefly wondered why Madame Lavoisier was being furtive, but forgot about her when he considered his responsibilities as the local gendarme. He believed that France in 1924 should be a safe place to live and his contribution to this security, especially on fine days, was to take a forty-five-minute bike ride from the HQ in Le Cellet to check up on the countryside and enjoy an excellent lunch at the café in La Place de la République in Forentan. Georges just wanted to stroll around the town; have a chat with a few people, tell off a few kids, move on a few beggars, maybe write down a few notes when someone was there to see him do it.

Fortunately, or perhaps unfortunately, the policeman had no idea why Marie-Pierre was concerned, as she always was when any official came to Forentan. Although ten years had passed since the evening when she had accidently killed her first husband, she lived in constant fear of the authorities finding out. Raymond Fischer hadn't died the same night that she clouted him over the head with an iron chair. He had woken up the following morning, but he couldn't see properly and when he tried to walk he toppled sideways. Marie-Pierre hadn't meant to hurt him; they had both been very drunk and were arguing when she lost her temper. A remorseful Marie-Pierre looked after him as best she could; they had no money to get a doctor and no means of transporting the injured man to hospital. Raymond seemed so get a bit better, but two weeks after he sustained the injury he had a massive stroke and died.

'Tu rêvasses ma cherie, on doit débarrasser les tables.' Bernard Lavoisier couldn't understand why his wife, normally so attentive to the customers, was skulking indoors instead of clearing tables, taking orders and serving food as usual.

'I'll go in a minute.'

'What's the matter?' Marie-Pierre sensed her husband's irritation. He was busy in the kitchen and had no time to do the front-of-house jobs that she usually did so well.

'Nothing.' She marched outside, going round the tables but carefully avoiding the gendarme. Inside the café, Bernard noticed her evasion. So that was it! He'd talk to her later; reassure her that she was not about to be arrested for murder.

The demise of Raymond had allowed Bernard to court Marie-Pierre, the woman he had worshipped from afar for many years. He waited a suitable time after the untimely death of Raymond before suggesting to his widow that she might like a job at the struggling *tabac* that Bernard owned in the centre of Forentan. Marie-Pierre not only transformed the café, turning it into the most popular lunchtime rendezvous in the area, but also Bernard. He found a new purpose to his life. Ten years ago he had considered joining the army, even though he was well into his middle years. Now he was the most successful businessman in Forentan, all thanks to Marie-Pierre.

'*Madame, un calva s'il vous plait.*' Georges smiled at Marie-Pierre.

She scuttled indoors. Bernard came out of the kitchen. 'Sit down, I'll take it.' His wife, unusually, did as she was told.

The problem for Marie-Pierre was that so many people had seen what happened on that fateful night all those years ago. She was ashamed of the spectacle that she and her late husband had made of themselves; these days she only had a small glass of wine before a meal, and the sight of a drunken woman was anathema to her. But then it was different; the Fischers were poor and desperately grieving for the loss of Marie-Pierre's son. Raymond had loved the boy as if he was his own son and each blamed the other for his death.

All this happened at the beginning of the war with Germany, and anti-German sentiments were high. Raymond had come from Alsace and spoke French with a curious cadence that sounded to local ears like a German accent. So when Raymond's wife walloped him over the head in front of a number of the town's citizens, no one really cared whether he lived or died. There was token concern for his welfare over the next week or so, but his death caused barely a ripple in the smooth millpond of town life. No one attributed his stroke to the after-effects of the trauma to his head, no one that is except Marie-Pierre.

Georges Hibou finished his meal and paid Bernard. As the gendarme set off to make his tour of the town, the somnolence of the afternoon was shattered by the unaccustomed roar of a motorbike. All eyes in the café were swivelled towards the lime tree where the rider propped his eye-catching machine.

'It's a brand new Peugeot,' opined one of the café customers.

'Cost a fortune,' observed his companion.

The stranger left his motorbike and walked purposefully towards Chez Bernard, taking a seat at an outside table. He removed his long leather coat to reveal a smart jacket and breeches, finished off with a gaudy cravat – city clothes that looked conspicuous in Forentan.

'*Madame, encore une bière si'il vous plaît.*' The request from a customer took Marie-Pierre's attention away from the stranger and back to work. There was still a lot to do.

Eventually she was able to sit down and enjoy a reviving tisane. It had been a busy lunchtime. Seeing the gendarme had reminded her not only of the circumstances of Raymond's death but also of something else that had happened years ago. It had all been very difficult. Her friend Christine Lemonnier was dying of cancer and she needed help to get her crippled daughter Amelie out of their upstairs flat and away to the convent. This had to be done without the girl's father knowing, as Christine was convinced that he would not allow her to go. Gaston Lemonnier had a bad temper and Christine was afraid to die and leave the girl in his care.

So one October afternoon Marie-Pierre had carried Amelie down the steep stairs from the flat above the milliner's shop and into a carriage hired by her mother. A trunk with the girl's possessions was tied on the back and the three of them set off for the journey to the convent at Louche-la-Mustique.

Amelie was very distressed when she realised what was happening. Her tears, pleas and sobs still resonated in Marie-Pierre's memory. It broke her heart to see Christine say goodbye to Amelie and leave her for the last time. Marie-Pierre's son had died of polio; she knew about the loss of a child.

Marie-Pierre wiped her eyes; these reminiscences made her sad. Today she had so much to be glad about; she must not let Bernard find her weeping. Come to think of it, where was her husband? She went to the front of the café. There he was, still deep in conversation with the young man who had arrived so noisily on the motorbike. What in heaven's name were they talking about?

She watched the two men shake hands. The stranger turned and strode towards his motorbike and put on his long leather coat. There was something familiar about him; Marie-Pierre experienced a wave of anxiety. For the second time that day she felt worried, indeed threatened, by the appearance of outsiders. She watched the motorbike make its clamorous exit from La Place de la République and prayed that she would not see it again.

Père Dujardin's Burden

Père Michel Dujardin was packing. After nearly thirty years as the parish priest in the little town of Forentan he was retiring. To be more accurate he had been told to retire. The bishop wanted a new priest to take charge of the town. He wanted a man more in tune with his own ideas, more committed to warning his flock against the sins of the world and saving their souls for eternity and less concerned with the day-to-day physical wellbeing of the poor and derelict members of the community as Père Michel had been.

The priest had already packed his beloved books into wooden chests. He had a few photographs and a set of fine cognac glasses that had belonged to his grandfather. He rolled these in old newspapers and placed them carefully in a leather valise. In another bag he put his few clothes. He was ready.

His housekeeper Odille brought him what would be his last meal in the presbytery. Some ham, hard boiled eggs, cucumber, an apple and bread. He ate slowly. In his mind he envisaged the faces of the townspeople from the last three decades; he heard their voices once more, shared their joys over again and relived their sorrows. One image stayed as clear to him in all its horror as it had done when it happened six years ago. He knew he would always feel guilty about the suicide of the milliner, Gaston Lemonnier. The priest also knew that by covering up the crime, in the eyes of God and of the law he too had committed a great sin. This part he did not regret; he knew that he would have to face his God on the day of judgement and he prayed every day for mercy, but he had acted according to his conscience.

It was 1918 when it happened. The war with Germany had just ended and France was on her knees. Poverty,

77

hunger and disease were rife. Influenza was spreading rapidly through France and across Europe; even in remote communities such as Forentan people were dying. He had buried so many victims of *la grippe*: young and old, wealthy and poor. He recalled the day when he had buried François Durand, leaving his widow to struggle with a large family that included her eldest son – home, alive, but seriously shell-shocked, from the front.

Amongst this misery were the on-going problems of the parish. The milliner was one of these. His wife had died not long after the start of the war, and his only daughter Amelie had gone to live in the convent at Louche-la-Mustique. She had been crippled by polio as a child and needed constant care. Left on his own and with a failing business, Gaston Lemonnier had turned increasingly to pornography for solace. His predilection was by that time well known in the town; fortunately his daughter in the convent was unaware of his shame.

Following yet another confession that had left Père Michel feeling soiled and corrupted, the priest had told Lemonnier in no uncertain terms that the only person who could help him was himself. That God loved him and wanted to help him but that he, Gaston Lemonnier, had to take the first step. Burn the photographs, books and magazines that he kept and not acquire replacements.

Lemonnier had evidently gone home, piled up all of his pornography in his backyard, doused it in paraffin and set fire to it. It then appears that he'd gone indoors and killed himself with laudanum. Père Michel found him the following day, the empty bottle of laudanum beside him and a telltale streak of reddish-brown dried onto his lips and into the stubble on his lower jaw.

The reasons why the priest cleaned the body, hid the evidence and told the undertakers that he had been with

78

Gaston Lemonnier when he had a fatal heart attack were several. Certainly Père Michel felt a responsibility, although he could not have predicted the outcome of his angry polemic on the milliner. Père Michel also considered Amelie; the poor child had the crippling effects of polio to live with, she had lost her mother to cancer, she lived against her will in a convent and he wanted to spare her the knowledge that her father had killed himself. He also knew that he would not be able bury a suicide in consecrated ground, and the scandal around the milliner was salacious enough without this additional shame. Père Michel had considerable sympathy for the deceased man, in spite of his addiction to pornography. As his confessor he knew about the abuse, the hostility and the shame of Gaston's childhood, so he took the sin of concealing the suicide upon himself, knowing that he would have to carry this crime to his grave.

Odille came in to clear away his supper tray. She too was moving on. The incoming priest had made it clear that he did not want to keep her. He did not want a woman with a child as his housekeeper. Dujardin gave Odille a small package.

'*Qu'est que c'est?*' She looked with some concern at the bulky envelope. 'Is it something I have to mend?'

'No, my child.' Père Michel thought of the bank notes in the envelope and smiled at her. 'You don't have to do anything. Keep it very safe and open it when I have gone. Not a moment before, you understand. *Pas un moment.*'

They were interrupted by a knock on the door. The priest nodded to Odille, indicating he wanted her to allow the visitors in. Framed in the doorway he saw Hortense Durand and her daughter Joséphine. Her eldest son Marcel followed them, hiding his face under his coat. He had returned home traumatised by the horror of the battlefield. Père Michel greeted mother and daughter before slowly

79

going to Marcel, taking the man's quaking hands in his old arthritic hands. Quietly he recited the Lord's Prayer. Marcel stopped shaking, so the priest continued with the *nunc dimittis*. When he finished, he invited Hortense and Joséphine to hold their hands as well and the three of them held the by now more or less steady hands of Marcel to recite the Lord's Prayer once more.

'This is for you.' Hortense gave Père Michel a small package. He opened it to find a scarf, knitted from wool that Joséphine and her younger siblings had collected from the fields and hedgerows, washed and then spun. Hortense did this every year to make sure that the family had hats, scarves and gloves for the cold weather. This one she had made especially for the priest. 'You might need that next winter. I don't suppose they light many fires in the monastery.'

The old man was touched by this gesture, and he had to agree with her, the room he had been allocated was chilly. 'I will treasure this always, and remember you all every time I wrap it round me.' Marcel was shaking again, so Hortense bade farewell to the priest and left.

Later that evening Père Michel looked round his bedroom for the last time, then sat on the narrow bed to re-read the letter that had arrived that afternoon. It was from Mère Agnès, the Mother Superior of the convent at Louche-la-Mustique. She was requesting him to prepare to administer the last rites for Amelie Lemonnier. The request did not surprise the priest; he had visited Amelie the previous week when he was in Louche-la-Mustique finding out about his retirement accommodation and he had been shocked by her condition. He had planned to visit her after he had settled into his new home, but this news made him realise that he should go to the convent as soon as he arrived in Louche-la-Mustique.

His last night in Forentan was spent in prayer. He recalled the words of Christ to Peter on finding him asleep in the Garden of Gethsemane, 'What, could you not watch with me one hour?' The hours of the night passed as the priest prayed. He contemplated his tenure in Forentan; many events had moved and challenged him but his thoughts kept returning to the suicide of Gaston Lemonnier. Now his daughter was dying; Dujardin had put his own eternal soul in jeopardy to keep any knowledge of her father's death from her and as far as he knew he had succeeded. He had covered up a suicide and deceived the temporal authorities, but he knew he could never deceive God and would ultimately be held accountable for this sin. It was a burden he accepted willingly.

The Road to Forentan

Bernard Lavoisier wiped his hands across his apron. That was close; he hoped that he'd got away with it and that he'd never have to see Byron Fischer in Chez Bernard again, but he doubted it. From the centre of La Place de la République he watched the motorbike splutter its way out of the town along the road to Le Cellet.

He had recognised the man even before the stranger had introduced himself. Smart clothes and cultured voice marked him out as a city dweller and immediately Bernard saw the striking resemblance between the newcomer and that deceased wastrel Raymond Fischer. After all these years, why did he have to turn up now?

His wife Marie-Pierre was hiding inside the restaurant. She was afraid that the gendarme, Georges Hibou, was suspicious of her part in the death of Raymond, her first husband. Bernard was sure that Hibou posed no threat. He was lazy and only visited Forentan when the weather was fine and he fancied a good lunch. He never looked for problems that might involve him in form filling – or even worse, making a decision. No, Hibou just wanted a quiet life, and telling off a few kids for scrumping apples from the tree in front of the *Mairie* was the limit of his impact on sleepy Forentan.

'You can come out now, he's gone!' he called to his wife, who reluctantly left the safety of the building.

'No he hasn't, I can see his bicycle.' She nodded to Hibou's push bike that he left propped against the café wall while he made his post-prandial check on the town.

'Not Hibou, I meant *l'homme chic*. I need to talk to you about him. Not now, later when it's quiet.'

'He looked familiar, almost as if I know him.'

Bernard said nothing; he had to think how to handle this situation.

'Come on, let's get the tables cleared and everything straight.'

The nights were drawing in, so no more sitting out in the square with a soothing tisane before they went to bed. So that evening they sat in the now deserted dining room, watching the last few customers in the bar.

'That smart city bloke is Raymond's son. That's why you thought you recognised him.'

Marie-Pierre put down her cup and stared into the tiny leaves floating in the pale liquid. 'Oh Mary, Mother of God. I never knew he had a son.' She got a handkerchief out of the bag she always wore across her bodice. 'Of course, I should've known straight away. What does he want?'

Bernard explained that Byron Fischer ('yes it is a strange name, an English poet apparently') had come to Forentan to find out about the father he'd never known.

'What did you tell him?'

'Just the simple facts. That Raymond did live in Forentan and that he died at his home following a bad fall.'

'You didn't say I was married to him?'

'No, I didn't mention you.'

'Thank goodness. Do you think he'll come back?'

'I think it's entirely possible.'

They spent some time discussing how to handle M Fischer if he did come back. Marie-Pierre suggested closing the restaurant and taking a holiday. They'd never had a holiday, perhaps now would be a good time to try it. But Bernard disagreed; he thought it would look suspicious. He did think it would be better if he spoke to Raymond's son and kept Marie-Pierre out of it. So they agreed that if a motorbike was heard in La Place de la République, Marie-Pierre would go upstairs and stay out of the way until he left.

In bed that night, Marie-Pierre thought about her first husband. He had loved her illegitimate son Clovis so much.

83

Now she understood why: her red-haired baby was a substitute for the child he had never seen. Raymond had not been a bad man, a weak one maybe, but not bad. And she had at the very worst killed him, and at best contributed to his death, by smashing him over the head with an iron chair in a drunken argument. And all this had taken place outside of Chez Bernard. Neither of the Lavoisiers slept that night.

Meanwhile in La Croix d'Or, the best and only hotel in Le Cellet, Byron Fischer was in a reflective mood. The wine tasted odd. Byron peered into his glass. He was accustomed to Alsatian wines; they had more finesse, more vivacity than the *vins de pays* available here in Le Cellet. But it would do. He poured another glass. He was glad he had visited Forentan and established that his father had indeed died there some ten years previously, though he was certain that the man who had told him this, the owner of a restaurant in the central square, was not being completely honest with him. He put that down to a lack of sophistication; no one in this place seemed even aware of the world beyond their little region. Not surprising, he surmised, they never go anywhere given the appalling state of the roads. He wanted to go home.

'You're a stranger round here.' A short grubby man in the uniform of a gendarme sat down beside Byron. He flung his battered overcoat onto an empty chair, clearly keen to find out more about the visitor.

Glad of someone to talk to, and relaxed by the wine, Byron introduced himself to the policeman and called for an extra glass.

'Ah, Fischer, now that's an unusual name round here. Not unknown but unusual.' Georges Hibou swirled his wine round the rough glass.

Byron hesitated, wondering whether to pursue this conversation but decided to change tack slightly. 'Not as unusual as my first name. My dear, late mother was a devotee of an English poet – yes they do have them apparently – called Lord Byron. She named me after him.'

Poets, English or otherwise, it seemed were beyond the policeman's sphere of interest. But he seemed intrigued by him and fascinated by his motorbike which was propped in the now-redundant stables behind La Croix d'Or.

Towards midnight Byron retired to his room in the *auberge*. He had gone to Forentan with only a slight hope of finding out what had happened to the father he had never known. His bourgeois grandparents had strongly disapproved of their daughter Marianne's clandestine marriage to Raymond Fischer. They had ignored him, refusing to accept him as their son-in-law and eventually he had moved away to find work. He sent money from time to time, and came home once or twice but eventually Marianne moved back into her parent's home, and it was there that Byron was born. She died when he was two days old, having lived long enough to insist on his unusual forename and also that her parents contacted Raymond to tell him that he had a son. They must have done this, because when Byron cleared out their house he found a letter, addressed to him and enclosing some money. The envelope was postmarked Forentan.

The story that Georges Hibou had told him in the old stables behind La Croix d'Or sounded too strange, too fantastic, too macabre to be true. If the policeman was to be believed, his father had settled in Forentan and married a local woman who already had a young son. Their stormy marriage had deteriorated into alcoholism and violence after the little boy died of polio. Hibou painted a sad picture of poverty and recrimination as the couple's fortunes went downhill.

Byron did not know what to make of the policeman's account of his father's death in the autumn of 1914. Hibou admitted that he wasn't there; he also said that in those days he never visited the outlying villages. They were dark and dangerous places, and the roads often impassable. He only learnt of Raymond Fischer's 'accident' some months later when everyone's attention was on the war with Germany. He told Byron that his father had been badly injured by his wife in a drunken brawl and died two weeks later.

'You said that his widow is still alive and that she married again?' Byron had carefully phrased the statement as a question.

Georges was in his stride with the story. 'You bet. She's a fine and successful woman now. Runs the best restaurant in the area. Her *cassoulet* knocks the one you get here into a cocked hat. She's married to Bernard Lavoisier, owns Chez Bernard in Forentan. It used to be a real dive.' He had paused before delivering his final bit of information. 'The story is that it was in that *tabac* that the Fischers got drunk and she knocked his brains out with a chair.'

A Roof over My Head

It's strange how things turn out. I'd never even heard of Passchendaele until the autumn of 1917. Père Michel told me it's in Belgium.

I tried very hard to stop Christophe from joining the army, I suppose I had a premonition that he wouldn't come home. But he'd made up his mind and even though I tried to stop him enlisting, I could see why he did. There was nothing for him here – no work, no future, just skivvying for that mean old Lemonnier. Ah well, it's all past now but I wish he was here.

The best thing I did was to go to the priest and confess what I'd done. Of course he had to give me a long lecture about thinking that I could deceive the Lord. All I'd done was to say that I was pregnant when I got married. It was a desperate, and completely useless, attempt to stop Christophe from joining the army. He enlisted, in spite of me pleading with him, along with Marcel Durand and off they went. They had this idea that they'd get free boots, free food, free medical treatments and see all the sights. What they got was lousy food, stinking old uniforms and horrible diseases from all the rats and filthy mud in the trenches.

Our little girl was born just a few months before he was killed, so he never saw her. I wrote to him to tell him that he was a dad and I got a lovely letter back. I've kept that letter safe and one day I'll give it to Jeanne-Christophe; she needs something from her father. She looks a lot like him, I'm glad about that. I wanted a photograph taken when we got married. There was a travelling photographer in town at just the right time. I got together a few francs and he took the photograph. I was so excited! He developed it in the shabby old shed on wheels that he called a studio, but when I went to collect it I was five francs short. He wouldn't let

87

me have it, said he'd keep it until he came back again. Of course he never came back, the war stopped all that. And Christophe only came home on leave the once, at the end of the summer in 1916. We had a lovely time together; that's how I've got our daughter. He didn't say much about what life was like in the army, just said he'd seen some terrible things and didn't want to talk about it.

Anyway, as soon as Christophe and Marcel had left to join their regiment at the start of the war, I knew it would soon be obvious that there was no baby on the way, so I plucked up my courage and confessed to Père Michel. At the time I was living in a horrible room in a lodging house just off La Place de la République; it was all we could afford. I'd lost my job and was just about getting by doing a bit of cleaning. Then I had a stroke of luck. The priest's miserable housekeeper left him. She'd been working for him for years, but it turns out that she had a brother in Switzerland and out of the blue she announced that she was leaving Forentan and moving to Geneva to look after her brother! Poor Père Michel was really left in the lurch and he asked me, yes me of all people, if I'd be his housekeeper. The presbytery is really big, so the arrangement was that I'd have the upstairs and Père Michel would have the ground floor. His knees are bad and he struggles on the stairs so this arrangement suited us both.

When Jeanne-Christophe came along he was a bit doubtful about having a baby in the house, but she's no bother to him. I think he's got quite fond of her; he's always giving her little treats when he thinks I'm not looking.

I've been a widow for seven years now. I was so very happy when we got married. But it didn't last long. Two months after the wedding Christophe left to go to war, and now I'm on my own trying to make ends meet. Even if I wanted to, I'll never marry again. There aren't any men left, simple as that. But I'm luckier than a lot of women, I've got Jeanne-Christophe and we've got a roof over our heads.

Lots of things have changed since the war ended but one thing that's got worse is the number of children begging and stealing. Not long after I started working for him, the priest asked me to make some extra soup. He wanted to feed some of these youngsters. Now it's quite a big thing in the town. Every day I make a big pan of soup with whatever meat and vegetables we can get hold of. Sometimes there's a lot, especially in the summer, and it can get difficult in the middle of winter, but we always make something. The baker gives us a few loaves and that's it really.

There are usually about two dozen kids at the presbytery door as soon as the church clock strikes noon. It's hard work, but you'd be surprised who comes to help out. For a start there's my aunt Berthe. She threw me out all those years ago when I pretended that I was expecting and now she can't do enough to help. Then there's my friend Claudine, I've known her for years. She means well but gets the wrong end of the stick sometimes. The other one who does her bit is Mme Gaudin from Le Manoir. I feel sorry for her. All three of her boys were killed in the war and her husband died of the flu. Now she's all alone in a huge house that's falling to pieces around her.

So I suppose it sounds as if I've got it all sorted out and in many ways I have. But one thing I've learnt is that you've got to look ahead. I want Jeanne-Christophe to go to school; she must get an education. I teach her what I know. She can read and write a bit but she needs to do it properly. I want to try to get her into the convent school at Louche-la-Mustique. I expect Père Michel will help me and recommend her but I don't think I'll have enough money. The other problem is even more difficult. You see Père

Michel is getting on and suffers badly from arthritis. When he retires, or more likely is told to retire, the chances of the new priest keeping me on are small. He won't want a child in the house, I'm sure of that. Also, I don't think the bishop approves of the soup kitchen. He doesn't come here often, but he did a couple of years ago when part of the church roof collapsed and he came to see what could be done. I heard him having a go at Père Michel, saying he was wasting his time and money feeding the poor kids. Didn't sound very Christian to me, but what do I know?

I asked Claudine, 'Do you think I ought to stay on here as a priest's housekeeper or move to the city and get a job in a factory?'

'You could always ask Mme Solange if she needs any more girls to work for her.' Claudine could be very coarse sometimes, but she was right. Many girls were forced into the game, they had no other option.

Aunt Berthe was equally forthright. 'You'd be stupid to leave here. You have somewhere safe to live, you have a job and you have good people around you. In the factories they work you to death, pay you little and treat the women like dirt. And who would look after Jeanne-Christophe?'

It was more difficult to talk to Mme Gaudin. She was after all a Lady; she spoke nicely, wore good clothes and had most of her teeth. But I did ask, 'Do you know where I might be able to find work if Père Dujardin retired and there's a new priest and he doesn't want me as his housekeeper?'

She thought about this for a minute. 'There's nothing that I can think of round here or anywhere else for that matter. Perhaps you could get a job as a governess or as a lady's companion. But it will be difficult with your daughter.'

'Odille, can you come downstairs please?' Père Michel only called me when he was unwell, so I ran down to him.

In his hand was a letter. Even I could see it was a formal letter. The old man's hand was shaking, he looked grey and gaunt.

'Sit down, *ma cherie*.' His use of this endearment was completely out of character. I knew something was up.

'I have received a letter from the bishop. He is planning a lot of changes and in his wisdom he has decided that Forentan needs a younger priest. He would like me to retire to the monastery at Louche-la-Mustique.'

'I hope that you will be happy,' was the best that I could mumble. I felt sick.

'The bishop has given me two months to make the arrangements.'

My mouth was dry, I had to force out the words. 'Does he mention your housekeeper?'

Family Ties

Byron had gone to Forentan with little hope of finding out anything. Now his head spun, he almost knew too much. Within the space of twenty-four hours he had established that his father was dead, but he had also discovered that he had a stepmother and that in all probability she had killed his father. No wonder Bernard Lavoisier had been economical with the truth yesterday.

Byron could see two courses of action. One was to go home, carry on with his studies and forget about the whole business. After all, he only had the ramblings of a stupid rural gendarme who had heard a lot of gossip. Hearsay wasn't any basis for accusing someone of murder. He considered his grandparents who had brought him up. They had had a very low opinion of his father, and never to Byron's knowledge had any contact with Raymond. He knew they wouldn't have encouraged their son-in-law to keep in touch, and they would in all probability have considered that whoever whacked him on the head did a good deed.

The other option would be to return to Forentan, ride back along that dreadful road and find out what had happened on that fateful night ten years ago. It would be necessary to talk to *le patron* again, and his wife. There might be other people who knew what had happened, but he suspected that they would all close ranks and not tell him anything. But he had to try; depending on what he found out he could then decide whether to go to the authorities about his father's death.

Sleep that night was out of the question. The arguments went round and round in his head. The length of time, the reliability of gossip, the reticence of Bernard Lavoisier, the stupidity of the policeman, the antagonism of his grandparents

92

to his father, the death of his mother, the existence of a stepmother, all contrived to keep him awake in his musty bedroom above La Croix d'Or. Before he left for Forentan Byron carefully checked his beloved motorbike: tyres, water, oil, fuel and brakes all working well.

Not wanting the sound of his motorbike to alert *la patronne* of Chez Bernard, he left the machine some distance away and walked to the square. He saw Lavoisier talking intimately to a woman. He looked at the woman he knew must be Mme Lavoisier with a curious mixture of interest and anger. He braced himself; it had to be done, he'd come this far.

The *patron* went into the restaurant, leaving his wife to clear some tables. Byron walked quickly up to her. '*Bonjour, Madame*, my name is Byron Fischer. I believe you are my stepmother.'

Bernard's plan for his wife to go upstairs if they heard the motorbike had been thwarted by Byron, and Marie-Pierre was caught on the hop. She had looked up from collecting plates and there he was, looking very much like his father, but with confidence born of upbringing and education that Raymond had never had. Marie-Pierre heard him say the words 'I believe you are my stepmother' as if from far away. She swayed and the young man helped her to a chair.

Bernard saw what was happening and hurried over. 'M Fischer. *Quelle surprise!* I did not expect to see you again so soon. But where is your splendid motorbike?'

'I left it by the church. But I fear Madame is unwell. She has had some startling news.'

'*Ma cherie*, would you like to go upstairs? I will ask Claudine to assist you.'

Marie-Pierre pulled herself together. 'I am fine thank

you. I must tell you Bernard that it appears that I am M Fischer's stepmother.'

There was no point in denying that Marie-Pierre had been married to Raymond Fischer. Bernard explained that he hadn't mentioned this when Byron had visited the day before as he wasn't sure then that he was actually talking to Raymond's son. They described the night ten years previously when Raymond had fallen down the stairs to their basement flat, carefully avoiding the subject of the drunken brawl. The Lavoisiers painted a picture of Marie-Pierre nursing him (which was true) and the complete lack of medical help (Byron could believe that; no doctor would come to this out-of-the-way dump unless the money was very good), the apparent signs of recovery and the sudden stroke that killed him.

The conversation turned to more general topics, and Bernard made his excuses, saying he needed to do a few chores, leaving the two Fischers some time alone to make small talk about Raymond. Marie-Pierre spotted her husband crossing the square towards the church, carrying a sack. *What's he up to?* she wondered to herself, but concentrating on not saying anything indiscreet made her quickly forget about what Bernard might be doing.

Byron didn't stay long. He wanted to get back to Le Cellet before dark. 'That road is appalling. Someone needs to do something about it,' he complained. Marie-Pierre agreed, but she knew there was no chance of that happening.

'Please come back and visit us again.' Marie-Pierre could be a convincing liar. 'If I can find any souvenirs of your dear papa, I'll send them to you. There might be a *cravat*; I'll see what I can find.'

Bernard returned, slightly breathless and uncharacteristically grubby hands, to bid farewell to their visitor. Byron gave no indication of whether or not he had been taken in by their account of how his father died. All he seemed to care about now was getting safely back to Le Cellet.

That evening the Lavoisiers had a rare disagreement. 'Why didn't you go upstairs and let me deal with him?' Bernard grumbled.

'Because it would've looked suspicious. He caught us by surprise and if we say we've got nothing to hide, then there's no reason to disappear just because he comes in. Anyway, why did you leave me alone with him? What was in that bag?'

Bernard hesitated very slightly. 'I remembered we needed some charcoal. Let's hope we don't see him again.'

'Hope not. He's clever, asks questions and never gives anything away himself.'

The next morning Marie-Pierre told her husband that she had dreamt of her long-dead infant son Clovis grown-up and riding a motorbike round and round in ever widening circles. Bernard reassured her; privately he shared her anxieties.

Towards 11.00, just as Chez Bernard was starting to get busy, *la patronne* was surprised to see Georges Hibou come through the door. Marie-Pierre no longer regarded him as her nemesis; she had realised that if she was going to be found out it would be by Byron Fischer not Hibou, and she greeted him warmly. '*Bonjour*, M Hibou. An unexpected pleasure to see you twice in one week. What can I get you? The *cassoulet* will be ready soon.'

Hibou's greedy eyes flickered. 'Madame, I come with bad news. There has been an accident. Yesterday afternoon on the road to Le Cellet, M Byron Fischer's motorbike hit a hole in the road. He and his machine were thrown into a tree, I am sorry to have to tell you that he is dead.' He

95

paused before adding with visible regret, 'And sadly the motorbike is damaged beyond repair.'

The gendarme sat down. Hearing the conversation Bernard left the glasses he was polishing and hurried across the room, a glass of cognac in his hand. Hibou reached for it but Marie-Pierre got there first, swallowing it in a single gulp.

Amelie at the Window

The train rolled out of Paris. Through the grubby window Amelie watched the crowded streets begin to widen and space appear between the buildings. The engine left the *banlieues* behind, picking up speed as it chugged and hissed through the countryside. Amelie watched small towns come and go, the train stopping sometimes for a few minutes, sometimes for up to a quarter of an hour, but each stop, each kilometre took her nearer to Louche-la-Mustique.

She had so much to think about, and thinking was an effort. She was tired and ill and she fretted about forgetting what she had to do as soon as she got back to the convent. Taking a notebook from her bag Amelie tried to make notes, but she found it difficult because of the constant jolting:

1. Write to Mère Agnès arranging that in the event of my death, some of my money is used to fund a place in the convent school for a poor girl from Forentan. The first recipient of this bursary is to be Jeanne-Christophe Pichon.
2. Ask if Mme Marie-Pierre Lavoisier could visit me as soon as possible.
3. Send a message via Mme Lavoisier to Mme Hortense Durand to tell her that her daughter Monique is well and happy and hopes to visit her soon with her husband.
4. Request for prayers to be said for the souls of my parents.

Exhausted by the effort of concentrating and trying to write legibly Amelie fell asleep, only to be roughly awoken by the train lurching over points in the ill-maintained track. It hurt so much she wanted to cry. The doctor in Paris had looked at the sores on her lower body and taken her temperature.

'This is not good. She cannot work, she must rest and maybe they will clear.' But Amelie saw him shake his head as he left the room; she knew what that meant. She had asked Monique Durand to call the doctor to the little flat they shared near to the Louvre. Monique had done her best to care for her, but she had been distracted by the upheaval in her personal life and had not given Amelie the attention she needed. This combined with the effort of sitting in a hard chair all day in the textile workshop had been too much for Amelie's frail body. When the two women had arrived in Paris only six months earlier, it was assumed that Amelie might stay permanently and that Sister Monique would return to the convent. In the event she had met an English journalist, fallen in love and was going through the painful and protracted process of renouncing her vows. While this was happening, Amelie was getting weaker and her physical needs were being increasingly neglected. Now it was probably too late, and her only hope was to return to the care of the nuns in the convent at Louche-la-Mustique.

Amelie watched the countryside become more familiar as the train trundled towards her destination. How she wanted to be off the train and safely back in the convent. She had made up her mind. She would stay in the convent for the rest of her life; she had seen something of the world and she knew it was not for her. But she could not take her vows; she had promised herself to Christophe Pichon and would not now renege on that promise and become a nun. She had sufficient money and other assets, as well as her skills as a needlewoman, to ensure that she would be assured a place as a corrodian, or lay pensioner, in the convent.

Marie-Pierre Lavoisier rang the bell that hung by the door to the convent. She heard it clang, the deep tones echoing round the sparsely furnished vestibule that lay on the other side of the door. It usually took a few minutes before a novice answered the bell, so Marie-Pierre had time to think about the death of her son Clovis. That miserable Gaston Lemonnier! She did her best not to dwell on what had happened all those years ago, but sometimes she just couldn't help thinking about what might have been. Her friend Christine Lemonnier had pleaded with Gaston to pay the doctor who attended Amelie to treat Clovis, but he refused *catégoriquemont*. It might not have made any difference, but then again it might have saved his life. So many died that year including Thierry and Rosalie, the children of Bernard Lavoisier who was now her husband. Amelie survived but she never walked again.

The novice who answered the door took Marie-Pierre to the Mother Superior. The two women had met before; Marie-Pierre had visited Amelie regularly.

'She is not well. I'm glad you have come today, I don't think there is much time left for her.' The elderly nun was clearly upset.

'But she is so young; can't you find a physician to treat her?' Marie-Pierre did not want to believe that Amelie was beyond help.

'We have tried everything, I assure you. We have made her as comfortable as possible. We use laudanum as needed.'

Amelie was pleased to see her visitor. Passing on the messages to Hortense Durand from her daughter Monique was a weight lifted from her shoulders. Amelie said she had been fearful that she might not live long enough to do it.

'Forentan isn't the same these days.' When she visited Amelie, Marie-Pierre always gave updates on the local gossip. 'Your father's shop is now a *marchand de nouveautés*; the new people sell everything from cloth and sewing accessories, knitting wool, and needles and pins to underwear and gentlemen's vests! None of the lovely hats your dear *Maman* used to make.' She saw Amelie's face fall and changed the subject. 'There's a new priest. He's quite young and wants to make lots of changes.' She didn't say that his housekeeper, Christophe Pichon's widow together with her young daughter, had been made homeless by the retirement of Père Michel Dujardin.

'Père Michel has been to see me; he's here in Louche-la-Mustique now.' Amelie seemed glad to have some news for her visitor. 'I saw him only yesterday and he told me that Mme Odille Pichon has been offered the position of companion to Mme Gaudin at Le Manoir. I'm pleased that they have got somewhere to live.' Marie-Pierre agreed and for the second time she did not pass on news about Odille. Everyone in Forentan was gossiping about the widow Pichon and the man from Pathé News. It seems that she had visited him in his hotel, *scandaleuse*!

Amelie was soon exhausted and dropped off to sleep in the middle of a sentence. Marie-Pierre looked sadly at her sleeping form; she noticed Amelie's brown hair, prematurely streaked with grey, tumbling across the pillow and the delicate hands that had created such beautiful embroideries lying translucent on the white coverlet. She knelt by the little bed and prayed.

Amelie opened her eyes just as the sun was rising. She could see its golden glow through the trees hanging over the convent wall, mellow buttery light heralding a beautiful day. By turning her head slightly to the left she could see, on the wall by her bed, St Christophe carrying the Christ Child over a wild river. The Mother Superior had moved the wall hanging from its usual place in the chapel and placed it where Amelie could see it; Mère Agnès understood the significance of this embroidery to Amelie. She also knew that it would not be away from the chapel for very long.

It had been three weeks since Amelie had returned to the convent after working as a *conservateuse* at the Louvre. She had seen tapestries, embroideries and textiles from all over the world. This young woman from a small town had never realised how many varieties of fabric there were, nor how the universal themes of love, death, fear and triumph could be interpreted in so many ways across time and the continents of the world. Back in the convent at Louche-la-Mustique it hadn't occurred to Amelie that it was odd that her embroidery of St Christophe should be hanging in her little room. She had sewn it more than ten years previously to assuage the grief of losing her mother and the realisation that she would never be able to marry the man she loved. Christophe Pichon had married someone else, joined the army and died at Passchendaele. Amelie always thought she had lost him twice, but the likeness she had created lived on in the wall hanging, and now she could see Christophe by her bed.

The sun was getting stronger; a sunbeam played on a gold thread in St Christophe's fair hair and illuminated the brown hair of the Christ Child. Amelie was aware of Mère Agnès picking up the long wooden pole with a hook on the end to close one of the heavy shutters, protecting the exquisite wall hanging from the rising sun. Père Michel Dujardin had been summoned by Mère Agnès. The old priest from Forentan had baptised Amelie; now he quietly prayed, 'Through this holy anointing may the Lord in his love and mercy help you with the grace of the Holy Spirit.' Amelie looked back at St Christophe and his precious burden. As she gazed at it she was aware of the pain in her lower body easing, what a relief! She tried to move her hips and amazingly they worked. She shuffled gently and wriggled her toes. For the first time in many years she could move her legs, it was a miracle.

With growing confidence she turned towards the image of the Saint that she had sewn with such adoration. As she did so she was aware of strong arms around her, carefully lifting her just as she had imagined Christophe Pichon would have done when she had dreamed of him carrying her out of the flat above her parents' shop and taking her to Lourdes.

She felt the cold of the river water against her feet and the wind blowing her hair. Mère Agnès closed the remaining shutter.

Afterwords

In this final section are a few letters and a newspaper report that give more information about some of the events and the players in the story of *Amelie at the Window*.

This short article appeared in **Le Journal du Louche-la-Mustique** *in October 1924. A copy of the newspaper was used as underlay for some carpet in an upstairs room of Chez Bernard, a popular restaurant in the village of Forentan. It was discovered in 1947 when the building was being repaired following bomb damage during the occupation of France that ended in 1944.*

The article has been translated and transcribed, as the original is very frail. The original newspaper is kept in the **Musée de la Vie Quotidienne de la Region** *in Le Cellet.*

Tragic Death of Motorcyclist!

Sometime during the afternoon of Thursday 23 October a gentleman visitor to Le Cellet met with an accident that proved fatal on the road between Forentan and Le Cellet. The unfortunate gentleman has been named as M Byron Fischer, a resident of Mulhouse and a law student of great promise.

Your correspondent understands that the front wheel of the motorcycle that he was riding came into contact with a large pothole, throwing the unfortunate rider across the road and into a tree. He had succumbed to his injuries before being discovered by a passer-by.

The new Peugeot was badly damaged in the collision and it is impossible to determine whether there is any truth in the rumour that the machine had been tampered with. A statement from M Georges Hibou of the Gendarmerie Nationale said that there is no reason to suspect any foul play.

Strenuous efforts are being made to locate his next of kin.

The original of this letter is in my possession. It was given to me by my grandmother, Jeanne-Christophe Pichon-Poussin. There are two photographs with this letter. One is of her father Gilbert Durand in his army uniform. My grandfather Gilbert died in Normandy in June 1944. The other is an older, faded photograph of a young man standing nervously beside a beautiful girl. At the bottom of the tattered surround is the name of the photographer 'Gilles Poussin: Studio Hirondelle'. They are my great grandparents Christophe and Odille Pichon. The letter and photograph were the only memories that my grandmother had of her father and they were extremely precious to her and her mother. Because it was written by a barely literate soldier in the trenches while the Third Battle of Ypres was raging around him, I have typed it out and inserted some punctuation to help readers.

106

To Odille, ma Cherie

I hope that you can read this, it is very dark and my hands are stiff with cold. I cannot write very much.

You have made me a very proud man. To know that our daughter has been born safely is wonderful news. I told all my mates and they wish us well. I wish I could treat them all to a drink to celebrate this miracle. But we need a different sort of miracle to get us out of this hell.

Please tell Jeanne-Christophe that her papa loves her very much and will be home as soon as he can. I am sure she is as beautiful as her mother.

Every time you look up at the moon remember that I am looking at the same moon. One day all three of us will look at it together.

Your loving husband Christophe

Early in 2019 Grace Downlands, a British PhD student researching the internationally renowned collection of embroidered ecclesiastical garments in the convent at Louche-la-Mustique, came across a box of papers relating to Amelie Lemonnier in the convent archive. Grace had spent some months working in the Louvre and recognised the name from the records she had seen there. She had wondered why all mention of Amelie ended abruptly in 1924; the convent records explained what happened to her.

The wall hanging of St Christophe carrying Christ safely across a raging torrent is still hanging in the chapel. Like so many people before her, Grace was moved by the beauty and integrity of the picture and astounded that it had been created by a very young woman.

The two letters that follow remain the property of the convent. There are no photocopying facilities in the convent so, with the convent's approval, Grace translated these letters that add to the story of Amelie Lemonnier.

Forentan
21 March 1918

To my daughter Amelie

I am writing to you because I need to
inform you of some matters of consequence
to you. It is entirely possible that I may
be called before the Almighty God sooner
than anyone expects. I do not tell you
this lightly, or to alarm you, but at my
age and in my current state of health it
cannot be long before I have to stand in
His Presence and accept his wrath.

To ensure that you have sufficient money
to keep you at the convent for the
remainder of your life, I have instructed
M Thierry Bougrier, the eminent Notaire
Publique in Louche-la-Mustique to ensure
that you receive 75% of my assets. I have
stipulated that the remaining 25% be given
to the convent to enable them to continue
to do God's work here on earth.

As you know, I own property and other
assets that M Bougrier will arrange to be
managed on your behalf. I leave the choice
of manager to him.

When your late mother, God rest her soul,
spirited you away to the convent I was
displeased that she had not consulted me.
I now realise that this oversight was due
to her rapidly declining health. It does
not excuse her actions but it does go some
way to explaining them.

My one regret is that I have not visited
you as often as perhaps a caring father

should, but I have never been comfortable
in the company of strangers. However you
are constantly in my devotions and I pray
that one day we will meet whole and
restored in God's kingdom.

Your affectionate father

Gaston Lemonnier

Louche-la-Mustique
5 June 1918

To Mlle Amelie Lemonnier

Mademoiselle

Following our meeting last week when it was my sad duty to inform you of the sudden and tragic death of your dear father, I am writing to confirm that I have arranged for money from your father's estate to be transferred to you forthwith.

I would also like to confirm that I have appointed an agent to manage the properties owned by your late father and now transferred to you according to his Will. M Claude Legros, the agent I have selected, is experienced, reliable and honest. I am confident that he will look after your interests with assiduous attention. The rental accrued from this source will be paid to you quarterly, less a 1% charge payable to M Legros and less costs for repairs and maintenance that he considers necessary.

Perhaps we could meet on an annual basis to review this arrangement and your assets? I will contact you in due course to arrange this.

Meanwhile I enclose my facture d'achat for services rendered as itemised*.

Veuillez recevoir, Mademoiselle, nos salutations distinguées.

Thierry Bougrier

Unfortunately the invoice mentioned in this letter was not with the papers kept by the convent.

About the Author

Penny Rogers is the writing name of Penny Dale; she uses the pseudonym to prevent any confusion with the marvellous writer and illustrator of children's books who is also called Penny Dale.

Before retirement Penny was an academic librarian, and in this capacity edited and contributed to books on learning environments in universities. She also wrote and presented academic and technical papers on learning spaces, as well as development and training for staff in higher education library and information services.

These days Penny writes mostly short stories and flash fiction and enjoys trying out different styles and genres. She has stories in anthologies published by Bridge House, Henshaw Press and the Dorset Writers Network. She is a regular contributor to CaféLit and has had stories published by Spillwords, Funny Pearls and in *Bare Fiction* and *Writers Forum*. She has been runner-up in the Mani Literary Festival competition and has been short listed for the Bridport Prize for flash fiction.

In her home town Penny facilitates a writing group that meets to offer mutual support and encouragement. She is also a member of a local poetry group and was on the management team for *SOUTH* poetry magazine until it ceased publication in 2025.

When not writing, Penny enjoys knitting, preserving fruits and vegetables from her garden and visiting historic buildings. She is particularly fond of old churches and is inspired by their history, architecture and continuing contribution to their communities. She is especially good at sitting in her beautiful garden, advising the gardener and planning her next story.

Acknowledgements

Many thanks to:

Roger Dale for the illustrations on the front and back cover
and for
Amelie at the Window (1914)
Outside the *Tabac*
The Way Out
Getting Ready for Bed
Fly on the Wall
The Legacy of War

Katharine Dew for the illustrations for
Evening Penance
The Power of Prayer
Forgive Me, Father
Secrets and Lies
News from a Small Town
Père Dujardin's Burden
A Roof over My Head
Family Ties
Amelie at the Window (1924)

Like to Read More Work Like This?

Then sign up to our mailing list and download our free collection of short stories, *Magnetism*. Sign up now to receive this free e-book and also to find out about all of our new publications and offers.

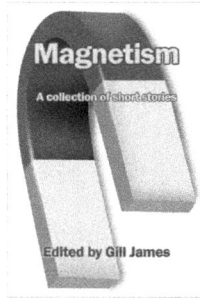

Sign up here:
    http://eepurl.com/gbpdVz

Please Leave a Review

Reviews are so important to writers. Please take the time to review this book. A couple of lines is fine.

Reviews help the book to become more visible to buyers. Retailers will promote books with multiple reviews.

This in turn helps us to sell more books… And then we can afford to publish more books like this one.

Leaving a review is very easy.

Go to https://amzn.to/45SWC0V, scroll down the left-hand side of the Amazon page and click on the 'Write a customer review' button.

Read More of Penny's Work in These Books

The Best of CaféLit 5, 6, 7, 8 and 13
Published by Chapeltown Books
(2017/18/19/20/24)

Order from Amazon:

Paperback: ISBN 978-1-910542-04-0
978-1-910542-17-0
978-1-910542-40-8
978-1-910542-45-3
978-1-915762-10-8

eBook: ISBN 978-1-910542-05-7
978-1-910542-18-7
978-1-910542-41-5
978-1-910542-46-0
978-1-915762-11-5

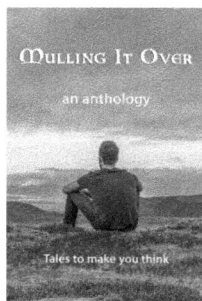

Me and the Bird in
Mulling It Over
Published by Bridge House (2020)

Order from Amazon:

Paperback: ISBN 978-1-907335-93-8
eBook: ISBN 978-1-907335-94-5

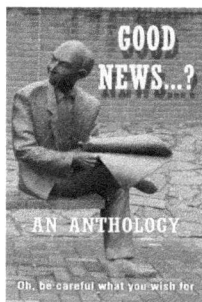

Cinderella Rising in
Good News…?
Published by Bridge House (2024)

Order from Amazon:

Paperback: ISBN 978-1-914199-88-2
eBook: ISBN 978-1-914199-89-9

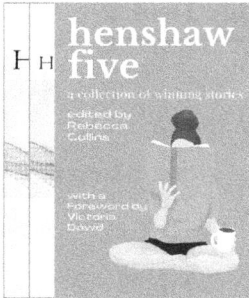

henshaw five

a collection of winning stories

edited by
Rebecca
Collins

with a
Foreword by
Vicotria
Dowd

Henshaw 1, 2 and 5
Published by Henshaw Press (2015/17/23)
Order from Amazon:
Paperback: ISBN 978-1-514690-32-1
             978-1-540766-53-3
             978-1-915817-20-4
eBook: ASIN B015NL3YSK
             B07171R3HX
             B0C75KMQPV

Other Publications by Bridge House

White Moon
by Mehreen Ahmed

White Moon is a collection of avant-garde short stories, micro and flash fiction.

Together they bring a stronger message than they do individually. The incidents in this book depict imaginary characters and events underpinned by dreamlike, strong surrealistic, even esoteric connections. The narratives bring together a unique blend of absorbing, entertaining and otherworldly experience.

As ever Mehreen Ahmed brings a strong and convincing voice to all of the texts. Enjoy the surreal and dreamlike quality of these stories.

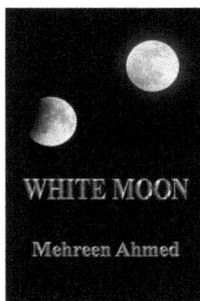

Order from Amazon:

Paperback: ISBN 978-1-914199-90-5
eBook: ISBN 978-1-914199-91-2

Once We Were Heroes
by Henry Lewi

Where do the gods of Olympus do their shopping?

Do the Old Gods live amongst us, and if so where? And which jobs do they do? Where do the Old Gods shop, or do they do it online? Which football clubs do they support? When Angels are sent down to Earth, how do they get home? How did Vampires cope with Lockdown during the pandemic? And finally, are Extra-Terrestrials dangerous, or do they just want to speak to us?

'Henry Lewi writes with confidence and with imagination. The story about the gods moving to North London provided an interesting opportunity to comment on modern times. The Pandemic features in many of the items in the collection.' *(Amazon)*

Order from Amazon:

Paperback: ISBN 978-1-914199-82-0
eBook: ISBN 978-1-914199-83-7

www.ingramcontent.com/pod-product-compliance
Ingram Content Group UK Ltd.
Pitfield, Milton Keynes, MK11 3LW, UK
UKHW022146070925

462690UK00010B/99

9 781914 199929